I0573349

Under the Skin

Vera Berry Burrows

Under the Skin

Daniel shifted uncomfortably in his seat. He thought carefully before he spoke. "It's difficult to know what to say. I am listening to what you are saying, but the words aren't coming from the woman I know as my mother. You're different, and I don't know why. I thought bringing BJ back into your life would make us into a family—something I haven't experienced before—"

Emma sighed loudly. "And I understand that totally, I do, but—"

"But what?" Daniel interrupted, irritated with his mother's assessment of what he had hoped would be a straightforward adjustment in their lives. "I didn't think there would be any problems."

"I somehow think you and BJ are wearing rose-coloured spectacles and I'm not. I've spent the past twenty odd years showing you that I can cope on my own, that *we* can cope without a father figure and I thought," she paused, "no, I *know* it worked."

"But that was then. This is now and we have the opportunity to begin again, to be a family like other families."

Emma shook her head slowly, trying to unscramble her brain. "Okay, I understand that, too, but we live in Jamaica and we have our surrogate family there, a family who has always been there to share our lives, ups and downs, highs and lows, whatever came along."

"Are you telling me you don't want to start over with Dad?" Daniel asked bluntly.

"I don't know," she admitted. "I honestly don't know."

"I don't understand you, Mom," Daniel stated with undisguised irritation. "A few minutes ago, you said you still love him. Surely love is what makes you want to be together, what will re-establish itself in all its glory when you spend time in each other's company again."

Emma stood and as she began to pace the floor, she instantly recalled BJ doing just that when she had told him she was pregnant. Forcing herself to return to her chair, she said quietly, "I said I *might* love him, Daniel, and that puts a whole new slant on things." She looked at the floor and without looking up, she said, "Apart from all that, there's something I haven't told you..."

What They Are Saying About
Under the Skin

This story deals with the challenges facing those seeking to rebuild loving family and personal relationships after a long period of separation and differing life experience.

Set at a time of changing attitudes to race and colour, it takes us through the struggles faced by characters, black and white, as they work their way through their own and societal prejudices. There are many twists and turns as the quest for happiness and self-fulfilment leads to a rethink of personal priorities and values, and an intriguing, unpredictable conclusion.

—Bob Corden, Mount Eliza, Victoria.

Author Vera Berry Burrows has skilfully spun a complex web of intrigue in this much-anticipated sequel to *Skin Deep*.

It follows the progress of Daniel, product of a passionate but doomed mixed-race love affair in unforgiving times, and the serendipitous events that throw his estranged English mother, Emma, and Jamaican father, BJ Johnson, back together. The story delves deep into sometimes fractured friendships and agonising battles of head versus heart.

Racial scars have healed with time; young Daniel has found true love with a Scottish lass and is on the threshold of a great career. The only thing he longs for is that Emma and BJ reunite to form the family unit he was deprived of growing up. Will relationship loose ends be tied? The author keeps you guessing until literally the last page. Another great read.

—Brook Openshaw, Bolton, Lancashire, UK.

Under The Skin is the captivating sequel to her beautiful novel *Skin Deep*, the story of Emma, BJ and their son Daniel. It is a tale of a mixed-race love that couldn't survive the scrutiny and boundaries placed on them by a society perhaps not ready to accept the love they had for each other all those years ago.

We pick up the story with Daniel who is now an adult. He has only just met his father for the first time and he hasn't told his mother. Daniel wonders how this will affect the close relationship he has always had with her. He hopes there might be a chance to have a proper family and dreams that the love his parents once had for each other has survived the years apart.

What will happen when they meet at Daniel's graduation? Will it be sparks of love, or resentment?

Vera has created strong characters that stay with you long after you have finished reading. It was exciting to meet up again with Emma, BJ and Daniel to continue their journey. I loved the storyline and was kept guessing until the very end.

—Karen Snowden, Pacific Pines, Gold Coast, Queensland

This is the revealing story of Emma's search for forever love. Her lead-by-example attitude and the wisdom of self-discovery see her looking for peace through the challenges of racism and colour, her love for son, Daniel and her first true love, Daniel's estranged father, BJ.

When Emma returns for Daniel's degree ceremony in Birmingham, England, she becomes unsettled on meeting BJ again after twenty years. Her growing lack of control leaves her feeling unsure of herself and she is torn between her love for BJ and her feelings in a new relationship in Jamaica, her adopted home. She has to make a choice, and Vera Berry Burrows keeps us wondering until the end of the story.

—Victoria Seedsman, Clear Island Waters, Gold Coast, Queensland.

Under The Skin, the sequel to *Skin Deep,* continues the passionate love affair of a young English girl, Emma, and BJ, a coloured immigrant from Jamaica. Set in post-World War II London, fraught with racial prejudice and a baby on the way, BJ can't handle the pressure and calls off their relationship. Reeling from the devastating break-up, a heartbroken Emma returns to Jamaica where she had lived previously.

Twenty-two years on, she returns to England to attend the graduation ceremony of her son, Daniel, who has engineered a reunion that leaves Emma and BJ both shocked and confused. Can they rekindle the passion they have both craved for all these years, or have they moved on in their different worlds?

Beautifully written by Vera Berry Burrows, the book has the reader riveted from the first page to the last. Definitely a book you can't put down.

—Carole Cullen BEM, Tweed Heads, NSW.

Under the Skin

Vera Berry Burrows

A Wings ePress, Inc.
Mainstream Fiction Novel

Wings ePress, Inc.

Edited by: Jeanne Smith
Copy Edited by: Bev Haynes
Executive Editor: Jeanne Smith
Cover Artist: Trisha FitzGerald-Jung

All rights reserved

Names, characters and incidents depicted in this book are products of the author's imagination or are used fictitiously. Any resemblance to actual events, locales, organizations, or persons, living or dead, is entirely coincidental and beyond the intent of the author or the publisher.

No part of this book may be reproduced or transmitted in any form or by any means, electronic or mechanical, including photocopying, recording, or by any information storage and retrieval system, without permission in writing from the publisher.

Wings ePress Books
www.wingsepress.com

Copyright © 2021 by: Vera Berry Burrows
ISBN 978-1-61309-522-5

Published In the United States Of America

Wings ePress Inc.
3000 N. Rock Road
Newton, KS 67114

Dedication

To Karen with my love and thanks for
always being willing to help.

One

Kingston, Jamaica 1950

Ann Brown enjoyed taking seven-year-old Glory and five-year-old Teddy to watch the big liners arriving at Kingston docks. "Look at that, kids!" she would say, and the children loved to see the ships as they moored alongside the quay. They watched in awe as burly stevedores ably caught and pulled gigantic ropes to secure the vessel so the passengers could set foot on Jamaican soil. Ann smiled as she watched the expressions on her children's faces and allowed her mind to wander back to the time when she and Emma had stepped onto Jamaican soil for the first time. *We must have been very adventurous, or just plain mad to do what we did while there was a war going on, but here we are, and we are very happy with our lot. I'll never forget that time seven years ago when Emma and I arrived in Jamaica with nowhere to live, no jobs and with the war still raging in Europe. I was four months pregnant with Glory and Earl didn't know I was trying to find him.* She sighed deeply. *It could all have gone so wrong, but look at me now. I'm happily married to the man who welcomed me with open arms. We own a business and a house and we have two beautiful children…*Suddenly she caught her breath as she saw a white woman struggling down the gangplank with two heavy suitcases. *Emma? Surely not…*But her thoughts were confirmed when her dear friend burst into tears as she approached.

"How did you know to meet me?" Emma sobbed. "I have never been so pleased to see anybody in my whole life."

Ann hugged Emma tightly and bombarded her with questions. "What are you doing back here? How come you have made this trip on your own? What made you come back anyway? I thought you were happy in England. Why didn't you let me know you were coming? I could have warned Leroy and Cherelle to have your house vacated ready for your return."

"I just need a friend," Emma cried. "My whole life is—"

"Oh, my word!" Ann interrupted. "This is not the Emma I know and love. Come on, let's get you home."

"But what about Leroy and Cherelle? I can't just demand they pack up and go without notice."

"You can stay with Earl and me for a few days and then we'll decide what to do when we have all calmed down and are able to look at the world through brighter eyes," Ann said tenderly.

Emma bent to hug the children and had to smile through her tears. "When did *you* become so philosophical, Ann?"

Ann nudged her playfully. "Since I met you and you taught me to look at life positively, and more to the point, since I had a husband and two kids, all with different needs. Now, that in itself makes a sensible, organised woman out of an inexperienced, scatterbrained girl. I learned the hard way, Em, but this isn't about me. You look done in and I've never seen you like this. Let's get these two home and then we can talk."

"Why is Auntie Emma crying, Mom?" Glory asked as they walked to the car.

"They're happy tears, baby. Auntie Em is pleased to see us," Ann told the curious child, hoping that Glory's penchant for needing detailed answers wouldn't further upset Emma.

"I only cry if somebody hurt me," little Teddy stated in hardly decipherable words, not comprehending how near the truth he was. "I laugh when I happy. I not cry."

"Come on, you two. Leave all the talking to the adults," Ann coaxed gently. "Get in the car while I help Auntie Em with her luggage." And then to Emma, "It looks like you packed up your life in these two cases."

"I might just have done that..."

Slough, England 1950

BJ Johnson sat for hours wallowing in self-pity. *Why does this have to happen to me?* he silently asked himself over and over again. *I thought I was taking control of my life. How could I have been so stupid to think allowing love to consume me would keep my feet on the ground?* He shuddered as he tried to work out what he should do next. *How can I face Emma after what I said to her?* Suddenly he stood and began to pace up and down, just as he had when she had told him the unwelcome news. This time he was calmer. He wasn't acting on impulse. *I have to work out what I should do.* He stopped abruptly and went to sit on the sofa, the sofa where Emma had thrown her coat just a few hours before. All thoughts of his darling Emma left him sad and confused. He sighed deeply. *I love her, I really do, but...* He shook his head, trying to sort out the jumbled workings of his mind. *There is always a but. It cropped up in most of our conversations when we tried to look logically at our situation.* He looked at his watch. *Ten o'clock already. Where did the time go? Maybe I had better sleep on the problem and my mind might be clearer in the morning.*

The next morning was Saturday, the day he should have been spending with Emma, snuggling up on the sofa, listening to the radio. *I can't listen to* Family Favourites *without Emma. I don't want to listen to anything we listened to together. I thought I would feel better this morning, but I don't. She told me to get on with my uncomfortable life without her. How could she say that to me? How could she just walk out and leave me? How can she just announce that she is pregnant and expect me to be happy about it?* He went to the window, still boarded up after the brick that had been thrown through his window on Friday afternoon had shattered not only the glass, but also his world. *I'd better get that fixed today; first things first,* he told himself and he prepared to call his landlord to find an emergency glazier who would fix the window as soon as possible.

Within the hour, he and his landlord stood watching the tradesman, and BJ tried to make polite conversation with the guy as he worked, but it was made abundantly clear he had no desire to talk to him.

"Do you find you are called out regularly at the weekend?" BJ asked in an effort to ease the indisputable tension in the air.

No reply.

The Polish owner of the property, Jan Bubak, himself an immigrant, replied as if speaking for the tradesman. "Most accidents of this nature happen at weekends when men...*and women*...have had a bit too much to drink." He shrugged in BJ's direction, discreetly shaking his head, and BJ necessarily read his actions as an instruction not to attempt to make conversation. BJ's thoughts of the glazier were less than charitable. *Don't show* *your ignorance, man. I'm in no mood to deal with your typical white superiority! Can't you see I have the same human form as you and probably a more tolerant nature? If you would only make the effort to know me, you will see I am similar to you in every aspect except the...*He didn't bother to finish his silent statement. *It is because of you and others like you that I'm in this mess.* He went into his office, leaving Bubak to deal with the guy to whom BJ, despite his resentful and uncharitable thoughts, was at least grateful for repairing his window at short notice.

~ * ~

The next morning, after a restless night, he slept in longer than usual and decided he would just stay inside, keep a low profile and do lesson preparation for the next week. He tried not to think about Emma, but not very successfully. *She was so angry when she left, and that's just it, she left. Should I try to find her so we can sort out the problem?* He sighed a long expulsion of breath from deep within his soul. *Maybe I'll talk to her at work tomorrow.* He sighed deeply. *But what do I say when I see her? I can't possibly entertain the fact of becoming a husband and father at this point in my life. I can't; I just can't.* He put his head in his hands and wept, for Emma, for himself and for the impossible situation in which he found himself.

After school on Monday, since Emma hadn't appeared for work, he decided he would take the bull by the horns and go to Castle Mews to confront his problems, to try to make her see the dilemma in which they found themselves. Nervously, he rang the doorbell at number twenty-one and waited. When the door opened, he saw a diminutive, silver-haired lady whose expression was thunderous. *This must be the renowned Auntie Edith,* he thought briefly.

"Is Emma here?" he asked quietly. "Please may I speak to her?"

The reply was accusing, caustic, derisive. "Don't you dare come anywhere near my house. I don't want your type here. What will people think if I am seen to talking to a...a bl...an immigrant like you? Get away, or I'll call the police! Emma has gone and I couldn't care less. I've had enough of her antics. With any luck, she'll see the error of her ways—"

"Please," BJ urged, interrupting the reprehensible onslaught from the angry woman in front of him. "Where is she?"

"I don't know and I don't care. Be off with you and don't come here again." Edith slammed the door in his face, so forcefully that BJ felt the ground shake beneath his feet. It was perfectly clear he was wasting his time. He knew from her onslaught that Mrs Booth would not communicate with him further. Sad and dejected, he walked away, resisting the urge to look back to see if the angry woman had had a change of heart.

After work the next day, he decided to ask Mrs Hopkins, the head teacher, if she knew where Emma had gone. "Why do you need to know, Mr Johnson?" Mrs Hopkins questioned.

"She told me she had some travel documents that might help with my geography lessons," he lied, not without realising that was what Emma had been doing for the past year, to her aunt and to herself, but, in spite of that, he continued with the deceit. "I thought she might be sick, seeing she hasn't been in school the past couple of days."

"She isn't sick as far as I know. Apparently, she has resigned," Mrs Hopkins told him bitterly. "She left a message with the education officer's wife on Saturday morning. I can't believe she sought him out at his private residence. She said her reasons were personal and she would need to resign immediately without serving notice. Very unprofessional, if you ask me. I don't mind telling you, Mr Johnson, I am very disappointed in her. She was such a good worker. I don't know how we shall replace her. I can't tell the rest of the staff or advertise for a replacement until I have official notification from the education officer. We'll all have to manage without her for the time being."

"I didn't realise she had resigned, Mrs Hopkins," BJ said, trying to look shocked but feeling he was failing miserably. The emotions deep inside were those of sadness, heartache and complete realisation that Emma was lost for ever. "Do you think she will have left a forwarding address?" he asked lamely.

Mrs Hopkins was surprised, even shocked, at his question. "Why do *you* want a forwarding address, Mr Johnson?" she asked haughtily. Then she folded her arms across her matronly bosom and took a stance that advertised she was about to give advice that shouldn't be ignored. "If I were you, Mr Johnson, I would leave well alone. You wouldn't want to blot your copy book, would you? I mean a Jamaican man chasing after an English lady..."

BJ felt like throwing caution to the wind and telling this overbearing woman she was out of order and had no right to cast aspersions about his character. "Excuse me, Mrs Hopkins, but..." He paused and took a deep breath. "...but I can see Miss Williams has caused problems for us all. I'm sure all the teaching staff will miss her. I think I'm going to have to buy a typewriter to type up my own lesson notes, and..." He paused again to regain his composure. "I'll find some other way of obtaining travel information for my geography lessons."

BJ struggled through the rest of the school year in Windsor. He put up a bold front and desperately tried to forget Emma, while his conscience constantly reminded him what he had done. He knew he had lost her because of his own selfishness, and he would have to live with that.

His friend, Devon became his sounding board and BJ was surprised when he said, "You know, BJ, you are too sensitive. Rose and I have put up with blatant abuse, but our love is strong and we'll survive. You should try harder to find Emma so's you can weather the storm together."

"I'm proud of you, Devon," BJ told him. "What happened to that brash young guy who arrived with me just over a year ago?"

"Rose happened, BJ," Devon said confidently.

"I envy you, Devon Harris, but I need to work this out in my own way. I'll move away from here at the end of the school year and hope the new start will show me the way."

"Are you running away, BJ?" Devon asked. "If you are, it's likely you'll take your troubles with you, or they will follow you wherever you go."

"That may well be the case, my friend, but too many things here remind me of the woman I love and the guilt I feel is unbearable. A new start in a new place might help me to rebuild my life. I have to try at least and deal with this mess I have created."

~ * ~

In order to make the break from his position in Windsor, BJ obtained a post in a Lancashire grammar school that would allow him to pass on his knowledge of the English language and his love of literature to pupils who had been selected because of their superior level of intelligence. He continued to work there until he left teaching to realise his dream of writing full time. He had already had his first book, *When Black Men Dare* published, and after the next book, *Angels Don't Have Black Faces,* he was unexpectedly, but rewardingly recognised as a leading authority on racial discrimination and social acceptance. He toured the British Isles, giving talks on the survival of ethnic minorities in a country seemingly not ready to willingly accept the immigrant population that had flooded its shores. Those were the people who, in 1948, had been invited by the British government to help rebuild post-war Britain, and they needed to prove their worth if they were to be accepted on equal terms with the wider population. BJ found some solace in sharing his views. He bought a cottage near Stratford-upon-Avon and the tranquility of his surroundings helped his creative juices to flow. Often, his thoughts drifted to the one he had loved and lost. *All this, the work I am doing, whilst inspiring, will never replace the longing for Emma within my soul. She has taken my heart with her, wherever she has gone and if I know her as well as I think I do, she will be determined that I should never find her. I have no doubt about that.*

Two

Jamaica 1950

Ann and Emma sat quietly as Ann drove home from the docks. Apart from prompting the children to behave themselves a couple of times, Ann assumed Emma needed to be left with her own thoughts for the time being.

When Earl and Leroy were over the shock of seeing Emma again, they went back into the workshop and continued to repair and service the cars and motor bikes that were bringing in their wages. Some of the local plantations were providing enough work to keep them going for years. New farming equipment appearing to maximise productivity was filtering through from North America, so Earl had taken a training course to learn how to repair and service heavy farming machinery. He was looking to the future when he hoped most Jamaican farmers would be able to afford tractors and the like, and eventually, his son, Teddy, would be able to take over the business when the time came for Earl to retire. With the help of his friend, Leroy, he had made the business flourish.

Leroy was particularly quiet after seeing Emma again, but spoke to Earl before he left work at the end of the day. "What do you think I should do, Earl?" he asked. "I mean, Emma was good enough to allow me to live in her home while she was in England, but a lot has happened in the past two years."

Earl pondered on the question. "If I were you, I would do nothing for the time being. Emma will probably stay with us for a few days, maybe weeks if she thinks you need more time and that will give you and Cherelle time to look around and find somewhere else to live. You could always rent a place." He grinned. "I pay you enough to afford rent."

Leroy grinned back and nodded happily. "The money isn't a problem, Earl. We have been saving since we got married, always assuming Emma would come back one day, but Cherelle is due in a couple of months, so the timing is crucial."

"Yeah, a lot *has* happened in the last couple years, like you say," Earl agreed. "But I know Emma and she won't see you out on the street, not like Ann and I were when she was expecting Glory. Let's just give Emma time to settle a bit and then we'll both talk to her."

~ * ~

Ann planned to make up a bed for Emma in the parlour. "I hope you'll be all right in there, Em. Earl made a trundle bed for Glory so's she could have a sleep-over with her best friend, Matilda—Tildy to everybody. I know it's comfortable because I slept on it when Glory was sick. I'll get Earl to push it from Glory's room into the parlour. You'll be private enough in there."

"Thanks, Ann," Emma said quietly. She was becoming weary and it showed. "Can we just have a cup of tea so I can tell you what's going on? I'm sure you want to know, and it will be a relief to get it all off my chest."

"When you're ready, Em, but yes, I'll put the kettle on. A cuppa's always a good cure-all." She smiled at Emma. "Remember when I told you all about my problems on the way out here? A problem shared and all that…"

They sat at the kitchen table while the children went out in the garden to play. Emma related the story about BJ and how much they were in love.

"I knew there was somebody out there for you, Em. You are too gorgeous to be left on the shelf."

"I became such a liar, though, and I didn't like myself, but I was so in love, Ann, and it was so overpowering and all-consuming and all I wanted was to be with BJ. He loved me, too, I know he did." She was gabbling, tripping over her words until she arrived at the inevitable information. "I'm pregnant." She burst into tears.

Ann went to hug her friend. "Don't cry, Em. Having a baby is wonderful and it will bring you so much joy."

Emma buried her head in Ann's motherly chest and allowed herself to cry out her frustration. When she had recovered, she felt some relief in finding a friend who understood and who was sympathetic. "BJ didn't want to know, Auntie Edith went into a state of apoplexy and Dad had gone into respite care, so he had no idea what was happening, but he wouldn't care anyway."

"Don't read anything into that, Em. Your dad has his own problems, from what you told me, so adding to them might not be a good thing," Ann said, trying to inject a bit of logic into the equation.

"You're right," Emma replied. "When I start to look at things more rationally, I will be able to assess my situation properly."

"And BJ might come round when he's had time to digest that he's going to be a dad."

Emma shook her head vigorously. "I doubt it. He was appalled at the thought of us bringing a mixed race child into a country that still isn't ready to willingly accept Black men in any way, shape, or form. Honestly, Ann, you have to see it to believe it."

"Oh, my goodness! I guess that puts paid to any plans we had of going back to the home country then," Ann said seriously. "We often talk about taking the kids to see where Mom was raised."

"I wouldn't go just yet, Ann," Emma advised. "I had to run back here because I didn't have the guts to stay and bring up a mixed race child on my own amongst all that bigotry and prejudice." She paused and then said, "That sounds like a coward's way out, doesn't it?"

"It sounds very sensible to me," Ann assured her. "You're not a stranger here and you know what living in Jamaica is all about. Yes, there is still some prejudice, but nothing we can't deal with. It really only comes from the very old people and the occasional teenage rebel showing his ignorance. In many cases, it's their stupidity that's out of control. Harsh, I know, but the new generations coming through should learn what people like you and me are trying to show them just now."

Emma smiled. "BJ and I talked about this a lot, but always came to the conclusion that we couldn't educate the world on our own. The least we can do is lead by example, Ann, and I intend to have this baby and show that nobody is defined by the colour of their skin. People need to learn that under the skin there is a person who needs to love and be loved like any other member of the human race."

Ann gave her another hug. "Oh Em, I don't know if the world will ever adhere to our example, but we're happy with our lot, aren't we?"

Emma smiled weakly. "I'm hurting just now. My heart is broken, but my unborn child will come into a world where love and understanding will overcome any problems we might face. I am very determined about that."

Three

Daniel Williams was born at home in Kingston, Jamaica, on Thursday, the fifth of October 1950. Emma fell in love immediately with the little brown baby as soon as he was placed in her arms. The attendant midwife had skilfully guided Emma through the birthing process in the comfort of familiar surroundings. "I shall be eternally grateful to you, Clara," Emma told her as soon as she was comfortable and Daniel was asleep in his crib by the side of her bed.

"All in a day's work, dearie," Clara replied. "I've told you before, my training in Wales has been a great benefit to many people here in my native land. My brother had been in Cardiff for only a few months when he told me about the training scheme. I had already trained as a nurse over here, but enduring the wrench of leaving my family for a whole year to go on that course proved to be the bravest and best thing I have ever done. The course was very comprehensive and there was nothing like that available over here at that time. I have heard, though, that better training is going to be made available to us in the not-too-distant future."

"You know, I have never been to Wales," Emma told her. "I came over here in 1943 while the war was raging in Europe. I returned to London in 'forty-eight, but came back here to have the baby."

Clara smiled. "I know there's a story in there somewhere, Emma, but it's your story and I won't pry, but you have a beautiful baby and it's clear his daddy is a Black guy. I just hope he hasn't sullied our reputation."

Emma, with tears in her eyes, smiled at her midwife. "No, he hasn't, Clara. This baby was made from love and he will be told who his father is as soon as he's old enough to understand. I doubt he will ever meet him, though."

"That's sad, isn't it?" Clara commented, "but it's clear he'll have some good and decent men in his life, judging by those two downstairs waiting with their wives to see you and young Daniel here. I'll tell them they can come up, shall I?"

Emma laughed. "Yes, please. I want to show my baby to everybody and there are little people, too, who can't wait to meet their baby cousin."

"Is Mrs Brown your sister?" Clara asked.

"No, but as good as," Emma told the surprised nurse. "I met her on my way out here and we have been very close ever since. She and Earl are my best friends and Leroy and Cherelle come a close second. I was able to compare notes with Cherelle while we were pregnant together, but her little Mikey is six months old now."

"Sounds like you have a nice little family unit there," Clara said cheerily. "I'll just go down and tell them to come up."

~ * ~

Six years later

"Why haven't I got a daddy, Mom?" Daniel asked when he was about to start school. "Glory and Teddy have Uncle Earl, and Mikey and Duane have Uncle Leroy, but I don't have anybody."

"You do have a daddy, Danny boy," Emma told him. "It's just that he lives in England and we don't see him. You have me, though, and I'll always be here for you."

"Why are you calling me *Danny boy*?"

Emma coughed to cover her sadness. "When I feel a bit sad, I always think of an Irish song that tells a sad story of a boy called Danny." *Oh Danny boy, the pipes, the pipes are calling*...she sang silently.

"Are you sad when you talk about my daddy? Do you think he'll come to see us sometime?" the little boy asked longingly.

"Probably not, son, but like I have just said, *I'm* here and I love you very much."

"It's okay, Mom. I love you, too, and we'll be happy with Uncle Earl and Uncle Leroy, won't we?" the little boy said, his mature understanding belying his young age.

Emma was taken aback. "We shall," she told him. "You have such a wise head on young shoulders, my son. Now let's sort out your things for school tomorrow."

~ * ~

By the time Daniel was eleven years old, he had grown to be a healthy, intelligent little boy. He attended the local school, which had benefitted from the recent restructuring of the Jamaican education system, and Emma subsidised his learning by using relevant textbooks from England. She had contacted her long-time friend, Mavis, whose own children were in school in London. As soon as Daniel had started school, she had written regularly to Mavis, the only contact Emma had with the home country. *Please, will you send primary readers and anything else you think might be good for Daniel's education? I've enclosed a cheque to cover the costs plus a bit extra for the conversion fee. I don't think there'll be a problem as the Jamaican pound is exactly equivalent to ten British shillings. Rumour has it we'll have our own currency here in Jamaica before long, so it might not be so easy to convert when that happens. Hopefully, I won't need the books by then.*

Emma, herself, established a business she could run from home. Her secretarial skills were providing her with a regular income. She started by doing an inventory for Earl's mechanical workshop and then he asked if she would keep his accounts up to date. News spread to the local farms and plantations who hadn't been used to keeping books and, as the number of employees grew, records needed to be kept. By the time Daniel was in high school, she began to look to the future with some enthusiasm. She obtained a position in a primary school similar to her post in Windsor and quickly became up to date with a Xerox machine, a vast improvement on carbon copies and blue fingers on a daily basis. Together with bookkeeping, whilst she could never be considered rich, she was able to live a very comfortable life.

She and Daniel were part of a close-knit circle of friends. As much as possible, she protected him from the negative vibes she sometimes sensed when they were shopping in uptown Kingston or when she attended school sports events. She often found herself on the sidelines with up to a dozen Black guys. More than once, she had become embroiled in what can only be described as a third-rate dispute about being out of place in that situation, which often ended in a minor fracas with other misinformed dads.

"Hey, lady!" one said with a wide grin on his face. "What you doing here? This is no place for a distinguished white woman. Where's your boy's dad, anyway? His dad should be here. We need people with Jamaica in their hearts."

Emma stuck her hands in her pockets and smiled at the guy with the chip on his shoulder. "I have Jamaica in my heart, big guy," she said in her friendliest tone. "I am not touting the colour of my skin in any way at all. Why would I?" She stared at her would-be aggressor, her inner strength giving her the courage to control a situation that might become ugly if allowed to progress. "Look at my boy. He's playing his heart out. I don't see any of your boys out-playing him."

"What you saying, mamma?" the big guy asked after one particular game in which Daniel had scored a hat trick. "Which is your boy again?" he asked, as if he hadn't asked a thousand times before. "They all look the same in team colours!"

"Exactly! My boy is no different from yours. I just see footballers out there, nothing to do with black, brown, or white. It might be worth you remembering that." Most times, the disputes ended amicably, but occasionally, the guys went moodily quiet and Emma was silently smug that she had made her point when it was needed.

She and Daniel had often discussed prejudice and what had happened in England before Daniel was born. "England was recovering from the war and the workforce needed to be expanded. They offered jobs and homes to West Indian people who were prepared to relocate. Unfortunately, the majority of English people were too ignorant to give Black people the respect they deserved. They made it very difficult for the immigrants to settle."

"But my father stayed when you came back here, so he must have settled," Daniel commented. "Why did he do that?"

"He wanted to establish himself as a British citizen and felt he had to do that instead of staying with me and raising his child..." Emma stopped to prevent the old wounds from opening again. "Actually, it's unkind of me to say that. He just wasn't ready to be a dad and he was unnerved at the thought of bringing a mixed race child into a hostile community."

"Sorry, Mom. I know you don't like talking about him, but don't I have the right to know who he is and why he didn't return to Jamaica when you did?"

"I have never hidden the identity of your father, have I? You know his name is Benjamin Joseph Johnson, BJ to his family and friends. Recently I heard from Mavis that he has become an author, but I really don't want to talk about him. I'd prefer to leave all that in the past. If it makes you feel any better, we were very much in love and you are the product of that love," she explained, not for the first time. "Knowing that information should make you feel good."

Daniel took her hand and squeezed it gently. "Thank you for reaffirming that for me. I'm not really bothered about him, anyway. I don't miss him since I have never known him. He's just a figment of my imagination." He paused and gave his mother a hug. "I love you, Mom."

"And I love you, son. An always and forever kind of love."

~ * ~

When the time came for Daniel to apply for a place at university, he approached the subject carefully with his mother. "Would you be upset if I applied to a university overseas?" he asked.

"Upset? No, why would I be?" Emma asked guardedly.

Daniel thought for a moment before he spoke. "I want to study social sciences and politics."

"What's brought all this on?" Emma asked. "Can't you study those subjects here, or are you thinking of going to the States? I'd rather you thought carefully about that. The social situation over there isn't always good. We hear of race riots all the time."

Daniel took a deep breath before he spoke. "Well, I can see how racial discrimination and social problems have affected the lives of thousands of people all over the world, not just in the U.S. I'd like to apply to Birmingham University in England since Birmingham, well Great Britain in general, apparently has a large immigrant population and it will be beneficial for me to experience that kind of life first hand. Politics will perhaps open doors for me to make a difference in the whole scheme of things."

"I can see you have thought deeply about it and I totally agree," she said. "That's what *I* needed before you were born—somebody to make a difference. I'll miss you terribly, but I want the best education for you, and in my opinion, there is no better education system than the British one. I'm biased, of course." She winked at him and grinned.

Daniel looked her square in the eye. "I'll be in England, though..."

"If you are asking if I'm concerned about you meeting your father, don't even think about it. Great Britain is a much bigger place than it looks in an atlas, so it's unlikely you'll bump into him on the street. Go for it, Daniel. I'm proud of you. Nineteen sixty-eight is your year...time to spread your wings." She grinned lovingly at her son. "Watch out, World. My boy is coming!"

Birmingham, England 1971

Time flew and soon Daniel was in his final year. He and his friend, Alison, spent a lot of time together and he trusted her with information he had never divulged during his time in Birmingham. BJ Johnson's lecture at the end of the last term had piqued his interest and he told her he wanted to meet the man who thus far had been a figment of his imagination.

Alison grabbed his hand. "Gosh, Dan, you certainly kept all that quiet. Fancy BJ Johnson being your father! I can't believe it. He's such an authority on racial prejudice and social acceptance. Mrs Fitzpatrick has even talked about his writing in our literature lectures. He writes with such dignified opinion."

"I needed to tell somebody, Ali, and I think we know each other well enough for me to disclose one or two personal details."

"Not too personal though, Dan," she joked. "Please don't tell me you're—"

"I need a sounding board, that's all," he interrupted. "It can't be broadcast, though, Ali. It would have too many repercussions if anybody on the course knew about it. Can you imagine how everybody would presume my views are the same as his? I could be regarded as his puppet—"

"Hold on, Dan," Alison interrupted. "Aren't you becoming presumptive yourself?"

"How do you mean?"

"Well, how can you say what others might think?" she asked pointedly. "They might not even care that you're BJ Johnson's son. You have a different name, anyway."

"Sorry, Ali," he said. "That must have sounded really conceited."

"No, it didn't," she assured him. "I know you well, and being an egotist is not your style. Mind you, when I look at you now, you are very like him. I never noticed before. What does your mum think?"

"I haven't told her," Daniel admitted.

"Blimey! Why not?"

"Because she would flip! She can't even read his books for fear of being reminded of the time she was with him," he disclosed. "Between you and me, I don't think she has ever stopped loving him, although she would never admit it. In all my life, I have never heard her bad-mouth him except to say he didn't have the balls to face public scrutiny in a mixed relationship."

"That's sad," Alison said quietly. "Do you think she would object to you making this decision without consulting her?"

"Probably, but I don't want to have more of a conscience about it than I have now. If she knew, I'm sure she would try to stop me contacting him. She tends to jump in the deep end without thinking about what is really involved."

"Then why incur the wrath of the woman who has cared for you and nurtured you all your life?"

Daniel sighed. "I know what you're saying, Ali, but I don't think, if she really thought about it, she would deny me the chance of knowing my father. I genuinely believe that."

~ * ~

BJ was already there, sitting in a private alcove just off the reception area. As Daniel walked in, he stood and moved forward to greet him. "Good morning," he said very quietly. "How are you?"

"I'm well, sir," Daniel replied confidently. "Thank you so much for agreeing to see me."

BJ signalled to Daniel to take a seat and then sat opposite him. "We met previously, didn't we?" he suggested.

"I don't think so, sir."

"After my gig at the university. Weren't you leaning against the wall as I left?"

"Ah, then you did notice me. I wasn't sure if I had imagined that you looked in my direction," Daniel said, somewhat shyly. "I didn't want to draw attention to myself at that juncture. The whole situation of your being there in the flesh was really a shock to the system."

"Oh, my goodness, am I so formidable?" BJ asked, nervousness showing in his laugh.

Daniel smiled back at him. "I have to ask," he dared to say and getting right to the point, "You do know why I needed to meet you, don't you?"

BJ looked directly at him. "Of course, I do and I wondered if you were going to punch me in the face for what I have done, or more to the point, what I have not done."

"I thought about it," Daniel admitted, not trying to hide his grin. "But I realised I needed to see where I had come from, how I evolved, if you understand what I mean."

"I do," BJ agreed. "I see a lot of your mother in your manner—confident and articulate, but without the..." He paused. "...without the bossiness I often accused her of in the early days."

Daniel smiled again. "I've been victim of that on numerous occasions, but she always capitulates in the end."

"Indeed she does...did," BJ agreed. "Is she aware of this meeting?"

"No," Daniel said firmly.

BJ looked sad. "Am I off limits? I have thought a lot about contacting you myself since that day I noticed you leaning against the wall. I felt a need to find out if the young man who has a startling resemblance to me was related in some way. Mind you, I wouldn't blame her or you if you have hated me for the past twenty years."

Daniel thought for a few moments about what he should say. "Hate is a strong word and I would hesitate to use it in this situation. She never shied away from telling me who my father was, but she didn't share her feelings, good or bad, about you. Only when I grew old enough to ask questions did she tell me that she would prefer not to revisit the past. I assumed it was too painful for her, but she never said so. She did make a clear request that I shouldn't ask questions about you. It was only when I came across your books in the library that I became more curious."

~ * ~

Emma had decided to fly to England for Daniel's degree ceremony and was very excited as she waited in her seat for the proceedings to begin. She looked to the left and then to the right...somebody was inching his way along the row to the vacant seat next to her. She wanted to run; she wanted to hide; she wanted the ground to swallow her whole.

"Hi, Emma," he whispered. "How are you?"

The ceremony proceeded and Emma sat in silence. She stared straight ahead, trying to focus on the master of ceremonies. Her mind was in turmoil. *I don't believe this. How can he possibly know that Daniel receives his degree today? I think I'm going to pass out. I can't breathe. I'm having a panic attack. Deep breaths, Emma, take deep breaths.* Obeying her own instructions, she endeavoured to breathe easily without allowing her neighbour to notice the panic that was overwhelming her. *Why is he here? Don't cry,* she silently told herself. *Don't you dare cry as you did when you last saw him.* Suddenly, her thoughts were angry and self-justifying. *But why shouldn't I let him see the devastation he caused? I still feel the hurt in my heart. Why did he do that to me when our love was so strong? Did he use me for his own gratification?* She checked her thoughts again. *No! Not BJ. He loved me; I know he did. But he sent me away, didn't he?*

BJ stared straight ahead, too, not daring to look into the eyes of the woman he had loved and lost, the woman who had borne his child. *How she must hate me. My conscience has been my punishment for the past twenty years or more. How can I expect her to see me as the person I am now? She accepted me when I felt most vulnerable; she loved me, I know she did. I felt it in all its glory...the love, the passion, the sincerity in her feelings, the acceptance.* Breathing in deeply and letting the air flow slowly from his lungs, he chastised himself silently. *Shame on you, BJ Johnson. You don't deserve her. You didn't then and you don't now...but I still love her with all my heart and soul.*

Still concentrating on what was going on in front of her and with her initial feelings of panic subsiding, Emma's thoughts became more rational. *I walked away and left the country. He didn't send me away. I ran away because I felt unable to survive amongst those who couldn't, or wouldn't, accept how I felt about my man. Was I young and irresponsible? No, I don't think so.* She dared to sneak a quick peek at BJ whom, she observed, was sitting upright, tense and looking straight ahead as she had been just a few moments before. Her heart skipped a beat, but she quickly became aware that Daniel was on the stage and about to receive his degree from the university's vice-chancellor. She roused herself, stood and applauded as loudly she could.

BJ touched her arm as she returned to her seat. "Congratulations, Emma." He smiled endearingly. "You have done well." He wanted to say, *my darling Emma, I love you as I loved you twenty years ago and I'll love you for evermore if you will let me.*

Emma stiffened at his touch but managed to say, "What are you doing here?"

BJ shrugged and studied his shoes.

Emma smiled at him. *Still the same endearing BJ,* she thought. *In spite of myself, I love him. I can't help it.*

They didn't notice when the rest of the parents on their row had all left their seats and they were the only two remaining. "Are you going to tell me what is happening?" she asked.

BJ shrugged, but looked up this time and took her hand. "I came to witness our son be presented with his degree. Same as you, I think."

She had not experienced that feeling deep within her soul for twenty-two years. "I feel like I used to feel on Christmas morning as a child," she said quietly. "Oh, BJ, what have we done?"

"What we have done can be left in the past, if you prefer," he said. "In my book, history does not repeat itself."

Four

Daniel found them still in a warm embrace and he tapped BJ on the shoulder to let him know he was there. "This is Alison," he said as he introduced the girl in whose company he had spent much of the past three years. "Alison, this is my mom, Emma and my..." He paused as he looked at his mother as though asking for permission to give BJ his natural title. Emma nodded and smiled, albeit quite meekly, Daniel noticed. "...this is BJ Johnson, my father."

"Hello," Alison said as she smiled at the two people in front of her. "I'm so pleased to meet you."

BJ offered his hand. "I'm pleased to meet you, too," he said smiling, the very essence of the smile Alison had seen daily for most of the three years at university.

Emma slid past BJ and went to hug Alison warmly. "Delighted to meet you," she whispered. "Are you and my son an item?"

Daniel stepped in and took Alison's hand. "We are going to be from now on, but we haven't been for the past three years," he explained. "Neither of us dared to say how we felt, because we thought we might get too distracted from our studies."

"Oh, my lord, Daniel!" BJ exclaimed laughing. "You must have been the only two students ever, who didn't allow their undergraduate libido to—"

"Hold on there, BJ," Emma interrupted. "None of those unseemly opinions required here."

BJ was appropriately censured. "Sorry," he said, as he shrugged and allowed his new found family to laugh at his expense.

Daniel laughed. "Alison has been the self-appointed spokesperson for me from way back. She has always championed my social standing in times of questionable behaviour from other people. I love her for that."

Alison's cheeks reddened. "Blimey, Dan, the L word has never come into our relationship," she whispered in his ear as she snuggled as close as she might in the circumstances.

He grinned. "I'll talk to you later about that," he said, and to steer clear of an embarrassing situation arising, "Let's go and have lunch. I booked a table for four at Jambalaya in town. I thought we might celebrate together, Jamaican style."

"What about Alison's parents? Are they here?" Emma asked.

Alison shook her head. "Unfortunately, they were unable to come down from Edinburgh mid-week. My dad is a surgeon and his ever expanding lists don't allow him to take his holidays at short notice. I did tell them as soon as I knew the date of the graduation ceremony, but..."

"And your mum?" BJ asked.

"She is a senior production technician for The Royal Edinburgh Military Tattoo. This time of year is very busy for her, especially since so many foreign participants perform in the

Tattoo these days. Daniel said I could share his parents for today, that is, if you don't mind."

"We don't mind at all," BJ told her cheerily. "Do we, Emma?"

Emma smiled. "If you say so, BJ, I can go along with that. How are we getting to the restaurant?"

"I'm hoping Dad has come in his car," Daniel said, as he looked questioningly at his father.

"My car is in the staff carpark. I took the liberty of asking Professor Lingard for a permit, seeing I am an honorary member of staff." He winked at Daniel.

Emma stared wide-eyed from BJ to Daniel in rapid succession. "A member of the university staff?" she asked in amazement. "How come I didn't know this before? Daniel, why didn't you tell me? How long has this been going on? Have you been deceiving me?"

Daniel breathed in deeply. "Relax, Mother. He's joking. He did an end-of-term lecture just before last Christmas. That was the first time I saw him in the flesh, but I *have* seen more of him during the past few months."

Emma looked accusingly at BJ. "Did you hunt him down?" she asked, and then to Daniel. "You were home last Christmas, but you said nothing to me about seeing BJ."

"No, I didn't, because I wasn't sure how I was going to deal with the situation at that point," Daniel told her. "I didn't want to..." He paused awkwardly. "Anyway, how could Dad hunt me down when he didn't know of my existence? Think about it, Mom."

Emma breathed in deeply, trying to remain calm. "I feel very let down at the moment, Danny boy. Why didn't you tell me you were meeting your father on a regular basis?"

"Maybe we should leave this discussion until later," he said, knowing that when his mother called him by that name, she was upset. "*Please*, may we have a lovely celebratory lunch like I planned?"

BJ caught hold of Emma's arm. "Please, Emma. Let's not spoil our boy's day," he coaxed gently in an effort to diffuse the situation.

Emma shrugged, cocked her head to one side and sighed with dramatic effect. "Well, yes, we have much to celebrate. Never let it be said that I'm a party pooper. Come on, lead us to your car, BJ. Things must be looking up. I remember the time when you only had the train to get you from A to B. I guess congratulations are in order for you, too."

BJ shrugged.

Emma noticed—remembering. *That's the old BJ. Shrug and the question needn't be answered. Nothing changes there.*

"My goodness, BJ!" she exclaimed as they approached the yellow Ford Capri with a black vinyl roof. "That's some car!"

BJ grinned. "If you can't beat 'em, join 'em!" he said jovially. "I could make a very inappropriate comment in light of our circumstances, but I won't."

"If it would be inappropriate, then don't," Daniel said. "There are ladies present. May I sit in the front with you, Dad? You don't mind sitting in the back with Mom, do you, Ali?"

"Of course not," Alison said. "I wouldn't wish to come between you and your big boys' toys!"

BJ opened the door behind the driver's seat for Emma, and Daniel opened the rear passenger door for Alison. The women slid into the back seat and made themselves comfortable. Emma quietly observed BJ as he drove carefully out of the university grounds. *Hmm, he drives well. Funny how this is the first time I have been in a car with him. Actually, this will also be the first time I have eaten in a restaurant with him, too. I have never really done any of the day-to-day things at all with BJ.* She breathed in deeply. *He was my lover, my soulmate, the love of my life, but I didn't live with him as a partner, nor did we do normal things together as normal people do. We were certainly not a regular couple.* She was deep in thought as they pulled up outside Jambalaya.

"Wow, Daniel! Did you book me a parking space right outside the restaurant?" BJ asked. "No yellow lines, are there?"

Daniel opened his door to look at the kerb. "Nope. No yellow lines. I guess we are just lucky, but we *are* on a side street. It would be different if we were on the main thoroughfare."

BJ parked the car and the two gentlemen opened the respective doors for their ladies to alight. A smartly attired young man opened the door of the restaurant. "Welcome to Jambalaya," he greeted them. "Do you have a reservation?"

"We do," Daniel told him, "Under the name of Williams. Table for four."

"Ah yes. This way, sir."

~ * ~

Emma was unusually quiet during the meal. She listened to the banter between Daniel and BJ and noted Alison's attachment to Daniel. She realised they were all very much in tune with the times and place in which they were living, all except her. She smiled to herself as she eyed first one, then another as the conversation progressed. *I have missed out on so much of this life,* she thought. *My roots are now firmly in Jamaica; my life is in Jamaica and here I am, a visitor, a stranger in the land of my birth. My son sits comfortably in the British way of life. The only physical thing I can totally relate to, apart from the obvious connection between mother and son, is the food on the table. What has happened to the English me?*

"Penny for them," BJ asked her across the table.

"Just thinking how Jamaican I've become. Somehow, my English heritage seems to have hidden itself away. I almost feel..." She stopped before she might say something too deep and philosophical for her three companions when they were all being light-hearted and happy.

BJ laughed. "Here I am, doing my very best to be the perfect English gentleman while *you* have become a Jamaican! There's a story in there somewhere."

Emma shook her head slowly. "Don't you dare, BJ. I have already recognised a lot of me in your female characters. I found it very difficult to see my worst traits recorded in black and white...no pun intended."

"Sorry, Emma," BJ said, his thoughts reminiscent of that time so long ago. *I wrote from the heart, my darling. Everything was very raw for a long time. My writing opened the floodgate for the wrongs I did you, and yes, it showed much of everything my life had become, warts and all.* He tapped on his wine glass with his spoon in order to halt what was threatening to become a public outpouring of his guilt. "A toast," he said with an authoritative air. "First to Alison. May all your dreams come true."

There was a clinking of glasses and quiet responses, "To Alison."

"Thank you so much," the young woman replied. She smiled at Daniel and he grinned as he nudged her playfully.

"And now to Daniel—my son, *our* son, the child I thought I would never meet..."

"Don't get sentimental, Dad," Daniel interjected. "Our meeting is part of this celebration..."

BJ continued unabashed. "To Daniel, my offspring, my soulmate, my joy. How could I ever make up the time I missed as you were growing up? That time is long gone, but we are here now and I hope the future you are carving out for yourself will include me in some way, however small or large. Good luck, fondest love, and best wishes to you for your future happiness and fulfilment of your dreams." He raised his glass, acknowledging the company around the table. "Daniel."

"Daniel," Emma and Alison repeated and they drank the toast to the young man who was Alison's evolving sweetheart, BJ's new found son, and Emma's little boy whom she had nursed and nurtured until he had grown into an adult of whom she was prouder than any other mother on this earth.

"Will you excuse me a moment?" she asked. "I need to powder my nose." She took her leave without waiting for a reassuring nod of the head from any of her companions. Once inside the ladies' room, she rested her hands on the wash basin and eyed herself through the mirror. Silently talking to the image she saw before her, she tried to sum up how she was really feeling. *What is happening here? The man I have loved for what seems all of my life has suddenly become an intrusion. How can that be when he is the father of my child? My situation in Jamaica isn't helping. I shall have to deal with that, if and when, but I don't want Wayne to be a part of my decision about BJ. I need to make that decision on my own. I am out of my comfort zone and I don't like it. I feel drained of all my confidence. Exactly where do I fit in?*

Five

When lunch was over, Daniel and Alison went off to celebrate with their friends, leaving Emma and BJ to decide how they might spend the rest of the day.

"I'm just slipping back to Halls to collect a few things. I'll see you at The Midland in the morning, Mom," Daniel said. "Don't wait up for me tonight. We're having a few drinks with our study buddies and I doubt if any of us will be in a fit state by the end of the evening."

Emma looked at him squarely. "I don't like the sound of that, but I guess you've earned a night of freedom. Be careful, both of you." And then to Daniel, "You look after this young lady, Dan. Don't allow a few beers to cloud your judgment when keeping her safe."

Daniel grinned and sighed. "Don't worry. I don't intend to get rat-faced, just nicely merry, and Alison will be completely safe.

When you meet the rest of the group, you'll understand that we are all there for each other. I promise you, Mom, there is no need for you to worry." With that, he took Alison's hand and they went off in the direction of the city.

For a moment, there was silence as Emma and BJ looked at each other and simultaneously shrugged. "What do we do now?" Emma asked. "I have no idea where we are and that puts me in your hands. What do you suggest? If you have places to go, I can mooch around the shops for a while and then go back to the hotel. Don't feel obliged to stay with me..."

"Stop all this jabbering, Emma," BJ said firmly.

Emma looked at him and pursed her lips. "Well, suggest something, BJ. This is home territory for you. I'm trying to let you off the hook. You don't have to stay with me if you have things to do."

They had taken the few steps to the parked car as they talked. "Get in the car, Emma," BJ instructed. "We need to talk. I'll drive to Stratford-Upon-Avon and we'll find somewhere quiet to have a long overdue chat."

"How far away is that?" Emma asked. "I don't want to be too far away from here."

"And would that be a problem?" BJ asked, uncertain why Emma was being so evasive.

He opened the door for her to get in the front passenger seat and then walked around to get in the car himself. "Are you happy to go to Stratford with me?" he asked pointedly.

Emma nodded, but her thoughts were quickly becoming out of control. *I don't know what to do. Why am I so uncertain about being alone with BJ? Being alone with him twenty-two years ago was all I wanted. What are we going to do? Will he want to kiss me? I'm not sure I'm ready for that. Will he want more? Oh, my lord, don't go there, Emma.*

BJ took the reins. "We'll drive to Stratford and go on the river cruise. It's a short but historically informative little cruise along the river. It sails past the Royal Shakespeare Theatre. I think you'll enjoy it."

Emma smiled weakly and nodded. "Sounds good," she said.

Once they set off, they were soon on the outskirts of the city. "We'll take the scenic route rather than go on the motorway," BJ told her. "You can remind yourself what the English countryside is like. Today the weather is perfect, at least as perfect as we can expect for an English summer day."

Emma smiled again, but did not reply. *This feels so awkward. All this small talk is alien to me, alien to us, to BJ and me. We were always so straight with each other, even when we first met.*

"Emma?"

The sound of her name broke into her reverie. "Yes?"

"Is something wrong?"

Emma looked at BJ. "I don't know," she said.

"What do you mean *you don't know*?"

"Exactly that, BJ. I don't know if there is something wrong. On the surface, this meeting today is the stuff of movies—*An Affair To Remember* springs to mind. Long lost lovers trying to make a memory come to life again; a clandestine love affair to be picked up where it left off; a romantic meeting supposedly to end all the longing and yearning for what has been missed. In real life, things don't happen like that. Actors portray imaginary characters and speak the words of the playwright, but people are real. *We* are real."

"What are you saying, Emma?" BJ asked cautiously as he steered into a lay-by to park. "If we need to talk so seriously at this point, I had better stop driving."

Emma sighed. "Can we go somewhere quiet where we can walk and talk?"

"This is quiet, or aren't you uncomfortable being in the car with me?" He didn't wait for an answer. "I didn't anticipate any problems, I must admit."

Emma was becoming ruffled. "Come on, BJ. We can't just pick up where we left off. I hope you weren't expecting that."

"I wasn't expecting anything, Emma," he said quietly. "As I made it clear to Daniel when we first met, I wouldn't have been surprised if he had punched me in the mouth for what I did, or didn't do, as the case may be."

Emma dared to smile. "He wouldn't have done that. I brought him up to respect other people regardless of their views and I told him that physical aggression never solves problems; it only exacerbates them."

"I wouldn't expect anything else from you," BJ told her. "We really shouldn't be sitting in the car discussing these things. Would you mind if I took you to my house? We could have a cup of tea and have our discussion in the comfort of my home. I live just down the road from here."

Emma bowed her head to hide the fear that was mounting inside. Her heart was beating fast and she didn't know what to say. "Ermmm…"

"Well, if you'd rather not…"

"I don't know, BJ. Can we just walk along the riverbank?" she asked quietly.

BJ was confused and it showed. "I don't know what is happening here, Emma. I'm offering a place for us to talk undetected, away from prying eyes. I would have presumed you wouldn't want to be seen walking out with me in public. After all, that's what we always had to contend with in the old days…"

"But these aren't the old days, BJ," Emma interrupted. "I haven't been in this country for twenty-one years. Times have changed; I've changed, you've changed, everything's changed." Her thoughts were in overdrive. *This situation has me completely bewildered. He doesn't seem to have moved on at all. Why is he still talking about us being seen in public? It seems he's still uncertain about a mixed race relationship. How on earth can we consider getting together with this big black cloud of division hanging over us? What price love, BJ? And what about Wayne? I can see it's going to be a choice...oh my word! It doesn't bear thinking about.*

BJ stuck his hands in his pockets and studied his shoes—leather shoes, expensive shoes—and his mind went back to the night he had met Emma in the Red Lion pub in Hammersmith. *I remember focusing on my shoes when she suggested we walk along the river. I couldn't believe what she was saying then and I'm not sure I understand what she's saying now. I am wearing more expensive shoes now, that's for sure. My whole life has changed, but my feelings for her are still strong. Why wouldn't she want to go to my home, the home I've made for myself while establishing a good life in this country. I feel I belong here, but Emma doesn't appear to share those feelings, in spite of her having been born in this place. And there's another person to consider in all of this, one I would prefer not to bring into this scenario.*

They sat quietly for a while, each with their own thoughts. At length, BJ broke the silence. "What would you like to do, Emma?" he asked gently. "We can't sit at the side of the road all afternoon." He paused. "Well, we could, but we could also find a more appropriate place to talk and have a cup of tea...and I don't mean at my house if you are uncomfortable with that suggestion. There are lots of lovely country inns where we might have afternoon tea."

Emma looked into his eyes and recognised the confused sadness that was seemingly bothering him as much as it bothered her. "I'll go to your house, BJ. I'd like to see where you live. You should be proud of what you've achieved, and I'm sure you are. In a weird way, I'm proud of what you have done over the years. We have a lot to talk about and I'm not sure a couple of hours will give us enough time, but at least it will be a start." She paused and breathed in deeply. "Home, James," she quipped to ease the tension, "and don't spare the horses!"

Six

"This is lovely," Emma said as they pulled up outside BJ's home. "It's right out of a *Country Life* magazine. You've even got roses growing around your door. Maybe we'll see it on a box of chocolates next."

"It used to belong to my agent's mother," BJ explained. "She passed away about three years ago and my agent put it on the market as is. I expected it to be very old-fashioned inside, seeing that it had belonged to an elderly person, but she must have been a very classy lady. She had the latest kitchen appliances, the most beautiful bathroom and the whole cottage looked like the interior designers had just left." He took out his key and opened the front door. "After you," he said, and he ushered Emma straight into his sitting room.

"Yes, I see what you mean," she said. "When I acquired my house, I needed to update everything. I was living in a demolition site for a while."

"I'll put the kettle on, shall I?"

"Yes, please. Do you mind if I wander round the garden while you make the tea? It's such a lovely day…"

"Please go and look at my roses," he urged. "They are lovely just now and I don't need to prune them for a while. I dead-head them regularly, though. Come through the kitchen and go out at the back door."

Emma smiled as she did as he suggested. "I see what you mean about the kitchen. It's lovely, BJ."

Stepping outside, she physically relaxed and took in a deep breath in order to compose herself. *I am so tense. I need to calm down. How am I going to talk with BJ like we used to?* She bent to touch a delicate cream rose from which emanated an equally delicate scent. *That's so beautiful. I would never have picked BJ as a gardener. It just shows how little I really know about him. He probably wouldn't believe that I have pristine lawns in my back yard. I take great pride in my immaculate parallel stripes.* She dared to laugh, albeit very quietly. *Well, maybe he would believe it since he used to tell me I was a perfectionist, especially when I insisted on my sandwiches being cut into perfect triangles. There is so much for us to learn about each other.*

Inside the cottage, BJ boiled the water and brewed the tea. *I have to make this perfect,* he silently instructed himself. *I so want to let Emma see how civilised I am.* He quickly interrupted his thoughts and checked himself. *Be careful, BJ. You are using distastefully wrong terminology under the circumstances.* He shook his head at his own foolishness and took his best china out of the cupboard, a Royal Albert tea set he had acquired with the cottage. He set out a tray complete with prettily embroidered tray cloth and called from the kitchen door. "We'll sit in the summer house, I think. Will you open the door, please? We can view the garden as we talk."

Emma saw a very pretty gazebo with wicker furniture and

floral cushions to match the curtains. A small table stood in the middle and a sofa against the rear wall, facing outwards towards the garden. BJ placed the tray on the table and went to sit on the sofa. Emma chose to sit on one of the chairs placed at each end of the table. BJ raised his eyebrows as she sat down. "You don't want to sit by my side, Emma?" he asked, without expecting an answer.

Emma shrugged.

BJ laughed out loud, a forced laugh, not a natural expression of enjoyment and Emma noticed. "Is that necessary?" she asked.

"Do you mean is it necessary to sit by my side, or that I should laugh at the suggestion?" he responded.

Emma was taken aback. "Oh, dear me, BJ. Do I detect a hint of sarcasm in your tone?"

BJ looked embarrassed. "I hope not," he said. "I always consider that sarcasm is the lowest form of wit…"

"But the highest form of intellect, so they say," Emma rejoined. "I didn't think your laughing was necessary in those circumstances." She felt her face flush and she lowered her eyes in the hope that BJ wouldn't misconstrue her opinion. "Shall we start this conversation again?" Without waiting for an answer, she continued, "This is lovely, BJ. Very English, if I may say so. I'm impressed."

BJ breathed in deeply. "Thank you," he said. "I do my best." He sighed noisily, leaned forward to place his elbows on the table and rested his chin in his hands.

"Elbows on the table isn't very English, BJ," she told him playfully. "I used to be told off if I ever did that. Sometimes it was a threat of no dessert if I didn't watch my etiquette! I learned very quickly to keep my elbows by my sides."

BJ removed his elbows from the table and clasped his hands together on his knees. "This doesn't feel very manly," he told her. "Will you pour, or shall I?"

"I'll do it," she said. "Mmmm, sponge cake, too. So very English!" She allowed herself to smile at him.

"Just so we are both on the same page," he said gently, "I rested my chin in my hands in order to formulate what I wanted to say. Your reprimand stopped me, so I'm not sure what to say in this instance. It's difficult to know where we are at the moment."

"We're in your summerhouse having afternoon tea," she teased. "Let's just take it as it comes, BJ. We can't plan a conversation like *we* need to have. Apart from that, I'm not sure I'm ready for a deep and meaningful discussion at this moment. What about you?"

BJ took a sip of his tea. "Baby steps?"

Emma gasped. "God, no!" she spat, rather more forceful than necessary. "We did that once before, and look where it got us. Raking up the past just now is not where we need to be."

"Forgive me if I'm being too bold," BJ responded, "but I assumed, obviously wrongly, that is why we are here. We have a past, Emma. We need to discuss it."

Emma felt her hackles rising. "Don't do this, BJ. Please don't do this."

He reached across the table to take her hand, but she snatched it away. "I'm sorry," he said. "This situation has escalated into something way beyond what it was meant to be. What do you want me to do, Emma? I really don't know, so please tell me."

Emma felt tears welling up in her eyes and she quickly brushed them away as they rolled down her cheeks. "I think I'd like to go back to the hotel."

"Are you running away again?" BJ asked, not hiding his shock.

Emma stood and made ready to leave. "Yes and no," she answered. "I'm not ready for this and I need time to think. Please, BJ, give me time to sort out my feelings. It's far too soon to talk about the future. We only just re-met a few hours ago. There is no way I can see where all this is leading."

The journey back was made in silence. Neither Emma nor BJ knew what to say and the atmosphere was sombre, yet not antagonistic. When they arrived at The Midland, BJ pulled into the carpark and switched off the engine. "Will I see you again before you return to Jamaica?" he asked warily.

Emma looked at him and seeing the devastation in his eyes, she took his hand in hers. "I'm going to the Lake District with Daniel tomorrow. We need to have some serious mother and son catching up time. We're hiring a car and plan to be away for a week. I'll give you a call when we get back. In spite of ourselves, BJ, you and I need to take time out. Too much, too soon might be our downfall and even I can see that we can't cast caution to the wind and pick up where we left off." Before she got out of the car, she leaned across and kissed him gently on the cheek. "I'll call you."

BJ watched her as she walked into the hotel. *Will you, Emma?* he thought sadly. *Will you really?*

Seven

BJ sat in his summer house alone and tried to imagine what was happening when just a couple of hours before, Emma had upped and run away...again. He was confused and told himself he really had no idea what was going on in Emma's head. *Was I misreading the situation? She appeared shocked to see me at first, but then she gave me a hug that hinted she was pleased I was there. She was quiet in the restaurant and then when Daniel and Alison left, she tried to get rid of me. She told me I could do my own thing if I needed to and she would look around the shops in the city. What was all that about?* He stared at the tray with the half-drunk cups of tea left to go cold when Emma had insisted she wanted to return to the hotel. *Then before she got out of the car, she kissed my cheek and said she would call. I couldn't read her expression at all, but I know I had a very strong feeling it was an idle promise. I am so confused. What do I do now?*

He pottered about the garden for a while and tried to unravel his jumbled thoughts. *If I concentrate on what we had before she ran away to Jamaica, I might remember something that would convince her being together would be good for us all.* When his telephone rang, it roused him from his reverie. He ran into the kitchen and snatched the phone from its hook. "Hi, Emma!" he said cheerily.

"Who's Emma?" the caller asked.

BJ pulled the phone from his ear and stared at it in horror. "Sorry, Gracie," he said quickly, and thinking on his feet, he continued, "She's a lady whom I used to know and who is visiting from Jamaica." *That's not a lie,* he silently told himself. "I was informed she would call me, but up to now, she hasn't."

"Oh, I see, and who, may I ask, informed you?" Gracie inquired. "When were you going to tell me about her? I wondered what you had been getting up to during the past week. I thought you were only in Manchester for a couple of days. I expected a call from you as soon as you got back."

BJ grimaced. *Get yourself out of this one, Mr Johnson.* "I was in Manchester until Thursday and then I've been busy and, although it really doesn't need to concern you who told me about the call, it was her son." *Not really a lie,* he again silently convinced himself. "Why did you expect me to call? You know I always take a few days to gather my thoughts when I return. Every lecture raises new issues, things I need to process for the next time I'm invited to speak to groups of people who are interested in the social ramifications for a person of a different race fitting in today's United Kingdom."

Gracie sighed loudly. "Oh, sweet Jesus, BJ, don't give *me* all that spiel. You're talking to me as though you're trying to impress me. I've been there, done that, and bought the tee-shirt. I went through the process of fitting in years ago, just like you. You don't need to impress me with all your heartfelt rhetoric. My job has been perfect for somebody like me. I've told you often enough and

I know you have used some of my experiences in your writing, so you must think there is something special about me. It's just that sometimes I think you don't take me seriously. We have been friends for a long time...it must be four or five years now. I like you. We get along well, but whenever I talk about taking our friendship to the next level—"

"Don't go there, Gracie," he said. "I like my single status and what we have is a really good friendship, which I appreciate. I like you, too, but I'm not ready to fall in love with you as I have told you many times."

"And you have always made that very clear, but I have to say, your words are open to interpretation, BJ. You aren't ready to fall in love with *me*, but it sounds like you might just be ready to fall in love with somebody else. There is something making you suppress your feelings for me, I know there is."

BJ's heart began to beat rapidly. *Gracie doesn't need to know about Emma and Daniel, yet she has always been so honest and up-front with me. She is always gentle and understanding, as goes with all in the nursing profession, but I have always made it clear I am not interested in her as more than a friend. I have never discussed the other part of my life with anybody, apart from Charles Winters, my publisher and agent, and would never consider telling Gracie. I know it would ruin our friendship— okay, a friendship with benefits, which puts me right at the top of the selfish list, I admit. I'm trying to justify my position, but I'm failing miserably. I have protected my heart from being broken again and I'm just waiting for a word from Emma to tell me our love has survived. That situation has suddenly become a possibility and the thought of being with the love of my life for ever, fills me with hope, and I haven't felt that for a long, long time.*

"Can I ask you something, BJ?" Gracie said.

"Of course."

"Will you give me an honest answer?"

"Of course. Why wouldn't I be honest?" He heard Gracie breathing in deeply at the other end of the line.

"Why do you make love to me when you're not in love with me?" she asked, with unusually blatant contempt. "You have rarely refused my attention when you know it will lead to sex."

Oh, my goodness! Think before you speak, BJ silently instructed himself. "I'm a man, Gracie, a man with needs. Any man would be a fool to refuse such an offer when it is handed to him on a plate. And I mean that in the nicest possible way. Do you really want to discuss our relationship in this way? You are cheapening it, and, may I ask, what has brought this on all of a sudden?"

"It's not all of a sudden, and you know it. This whole sorry situation has filled my thoughts, particularly while you were away this time, and I have decided I need some stability in my life." She paused for a moment and then, realising what he had said about being handed sex on a plate, she snapped, "Are you saying I'm easy?"

"No, I'm not. I love you as a friend, but I'm not in love with you."

Gracie continued unabashed. "There is a very fine line between loving and being in love. You seem to have a clear understanding of it, but I don't. I have wanted to have this conversation with you on numerous occasions over the years, but I always decided to leave well alone. I like you, BJ...I like you a lot and I would even venture to say I'm in love with you. Sometimes I feel I will burst if I can't show you and tell you honestly how I feel, but we never seem to find the time to discuss our feelings for each other in that way."

"That's because we are comfortable in each other's company," BJ explained, still with measured caution. "Why would we spoil that by saying what I think is unnecessary in our case?" But his thoughts were becoming jumbled. *I am digging such a deep hole for myself. I am becoming a fool and not owning up to the fact that my heart lies with Emma, the woman I am hoping will rekindle the love we had for each other before it all went horribly wrong.* "Can we talk about this later, Gracie?" I am up to a delicate part in my novel and I need to be able to write it sensitively..." *I am lying! Oh lord, not again.*

"That's all part of it, BJ. Knowing how sensitive you are, I didn't want to rock the boat. It has always been a *don't-try-to-fix-what-isn't-broken* situation, so I kept quiet. Well, now I've made a decision and you may not like it. Either you make this relationship more permanent, or I'll not see you again. A girl can't spend her whole life waiting around for a guy who just wants her when he feels like a bit of—"

"Hold on there, Gracie," BJ interrupted. "It's not like that and you know it. I would never treat a woman in that way. I enjoy your company and we don't end up in bed every time I see you. Our relationship is better than that."

"But you never allow me to stay overnight and I have suggested more than once that I should move in with you. We're good together, BJ. We make a lovely couple. We match...we are both—"

"Stop this, Gracie. I'm not in the mood to get into a deep and meaningful conversation about the rights and wrongs of our relationship," BJ told her firmly while telling himself silently, *I am allowing myself to be irritated and it's not Gracie's fault. I know I'm being selfish, but I can't help it.* "Why are you rocking the boat now?"

"That's typical of you, BJ. For a writer of deep and meaningful novels, you ought to be able to openly discuss your innermost feelings. When it comes to talking about yourself, you are a closed book, no pun intended."

BJ shrugged and then silently chastised himself. *Nobody to see the shrug, BJ. Wasn't it Emma who told you first about shrugging when you didn't quite know how to answer a question or comment?* "Not now, Gracie. I'll call you later."

"Well, I won't hold my breath, BJ. If I don't hear from you by next weekend, I'll know what to do for my own sanity," Gracie told him. "I'm working nights this week, but I'll be round there again next Saturday for you to give me an answer one way or the other."

~ * ~

In order to dismiss Gracie's threat, albeit a mild threat, from his mind, BJ spent the next couple of days on a new project and immersed himself in the brainstorming that was always the precursor to his writing. *Lost and Found* gave him the escape from reality for a while until he realised he was writing something which was becoming too autobiographical and he instantly came down to earth with a bang. *Emma, Emma, Emma, what are you doing to me again? You are making me feel so insecure.* He banged his fist hard on the desk. *I need to feel and show the love I have deep within my soul and, selfish though it may seem, I think I'll phone Gracie. I know she will make me feel good.* He picked up the phone, looked at it and then forcefully replaced it on the hook without making the call. He returned to his study, asking himself silently, *who are you? What have you become? You are a parody of your former self. Sort yourself out.*

Eight

After leaving Emma and BJ at the restaurant, Daniel and Alison partied the night away and wandered back to The Midland Hotel at three in the morning. Emma had booked a room for Daniel so that they might make an early start setting off on their trip to The Lakes the following day.

"I'll wait for Alexa here in reception," Alison said. "She shouldn't be long and her flat is only round the corner from here. You go up, Dan. I'll be okay."

"I wouldn't dream of leaving you here on your own," he told her. "She might be ages. I saw her wrapped in Lenny's arms just before we left. Let's sit in this alcove. If we fall asleep, it won't matter." He put his arm around her and she rested her head on his shoulder. His heart leapt in his chest not for the first time that evening and his thoughts were running riot. *I kissed this girl for the first time earlier and my head spun. Feeling her so close to me now makes me realise how much I love her, how much I want her.* He tilted her head so that he might kiss her again. Their lips met and each felt the other's longing. Daniel took a deep breath and holding her close, he whispered in her ear. "Stay with me tonight, Ali."

Alison looked into his eyes, eyes that told her he loved her. "What about Alexa? She thinks I'm staying with her."

Daniel thought for a moment. "We'll leave a message at the reception desk to let her know you are staying here. If I know them as well as I think I do, both she and Lenny will go back to her flat and if you are here with me, you won't have to play gooseberry." He kissed her again and felt her gentle submission at his touch. "I love you," he whispered.

"I love you too," she told him quietly. "So, so much."

~ * ~

Emma was the first down to breakfast and was surprised when Daniel walked into the dining room with Alison. "Good morning," she said, and looked questioningly at her son.

"Good morning, Mom. Did you sleep well?" He knew she was more than curious about Alison being there, but he chose not to enlighten her.

Tacitly taking the point, Emma replied. "Not very well, if I'm honest. I had so much going round and round in my head. Nothing for you to worry about, though. Nice to see you again, Alison."

"And you," Alison said. "I hope you don't mind me having breakfast with you."

"Of course not," Emma reassured her. "But you do know that Daniel and I are going off to The Lakes soon after breakfast?"

Daniel jumped in. "She does know, and she can come with us as far as Kendal and then catch a train home to Edinburgh from there."

"Will that be okay, Mrs..." Alison blushed and looked at Daniel for support.

"*Emma* will do," he said, and waited for his mother's approval.

"Of course," Emma agreed.

Alison smiled with relief. "The train takes just over two hours from Kendal and I must say, the fare is only half of what it would be if I travelled to Edinburgh from Birmingham. I'm still able to get student rates, thank goodness."

"Are your parents expecting you today?" Emma asked.

"They are, and Mum will be at the station to pick me up," Alison explained. "I'll have a couple of weeks at home and then I have to be back over the border in Liverpool in time for the start of term. I have a teaching post in a Merseyside school and I still have to find somewhere to live."

"My goodness," Emma exclaimed. "You *are* going to be busy."

"She is," Daniel chipped in. "No time for me for just over a week, but we can discuss all this later. Let's eat and then we'll pick up Ali's stuff from Alexa's flat and be on our way."

~ * ~

The hire car was perfect. The Ford Cortina was small enough to handle easily and large enough to allow passenger comfort. Daniel drove and Emma sat in the back so Alison might feel close to Daniel as far as Kendal. Emma rested her head on the back of her seat and closed her eyes. She needed to relax and think through what had happened with BJ the day before. She sighed deeply.

"Are we keeping you awake, Mom?" Daniel called from the driver's seat.

"Just taking in the air so I can rest easy for a while," she explained. "Drive carefully, Daniel. You have two ladies to keep safe, you know."

"I know. Don't worry. My driving instructor was an excellent driver and taught me well."

"I know that," she said. "The best!"

Alison was amused by their little scenario. "I'm guessing you taught him to drive, Emma."

"I did indeed, and I'm confident I can rely on him to get us all there in one piece." She closed her eyes again and felt the smooth running of the car helping her to relax. *I can't believe all that has happened in the last twenty-four hours. Seeing BJ again yesterday was totally unexpected. How am I supposed to feel? Initially, it was wonderful—strange, but wonderful in its own way. When reality set in, I didn't know how I felt. I still don't. I'm confused, utterly confused. He's still the same BJ, endearingly attentive and considerate. I have clung to the memories of him for the past twenty years and now that he's in my life again...*She questioned herself abruptly. *In my life? Is he? Do I really mean that? Oh, my lord! I have so much to sort out. One car journey isn't going to do it and I'm only here in England for a couple of weeks...*She sighed deeply. *And what about Wayne?*

Emma opened her eyes with a start as the car stopped. "Wake up, Mom. We're in Kendal and I'm going to take Ali into the station," Daniel told her. "Are you coming in with us..."

"And feel like a spare part?" Emma said, laughing. "No, I'll stay here and maybe stretch my legs in a little while. Have a safe trip, Alison. Lovely to meet you and no doubt I'll see you again before I go back to Jamaica."

"I'll try," Alison replied, "although Mum and Dad are expecting me to spend most of my time with them, seeing that I'll be living in Liverpool when the new school term begins. I really will try, Emma, and I have to tell them about Dan and me, especially since we'll be living..."

"...we'll be more settled as a couple by the time I get to meet them," Daniel interrupted. "Come on, Ali. You're going to miss your train if we hang around here much longer."

"Okay," Alison agreed. "See you later, Emma."

As the young couple walked quickly towards the station entrance, Emma realised she hadn't been told the whole story.

Hmmm, she thought, *I think I'm missing something with those two. Daniel was quick to stop Alison in her tracks just then.*

~ * ~

The train was waiting in the station as they ran down the steps to platform one. Daniel helped Alison with her luggage and wound down the carriage window so he might kiss her one last time before she left. "I'll miss you," he told her. "More than you know."

"I'll miss you, too," she said. "I'll wait for you to call when you can drag yourself away from your mum for a minute or two."

"I'll just be honest with her," Daniel said firmly. "I wouldn't dream of making excuses just to make a phone call. She'd know if I did. I'm sure she was a clairvoyant in a former life!"

Alison laughed. "I love your honesty, Dan. It's one of the many things I adore about you."

Daniel took her face in his hands and kissed her tenderly on the lips as the guard's whistle blew, informing them the train was about to leave. "Take care, Ali. The next seven days will drag for me without you."

"No, they won't," she told him. "You and your mum will have a great time. You'll love the Lake District. There is so much to see and do. You won't have time to think of me."

"Wanna bet?"

She smiled as the train pulled out of the station. "Call me tonight," she said.

"Will do." And he stood on the platform waving goodbye until Alison and the train disappeared in the distance.

~ * ~

Emma was already sitting in the front passenger seat when Daniel returned to the car. "Alison caught her train in time?" she asked, not really needing an answer.

"She did and we should be in Windermere in less than an hour," he said cheerily. "Would you like to drive, or are you willing to be a passenger for the rest of the trip?"

"You can drive," Emma told him. "I quite like being chauffeur driven for a change. It doesn't happen very often."

"Not a problem," Daniel replied. "It's a nice change for me, too, to be able to drive. I have missed having a car while I've been at uni."

Emma looked at her son, who appeared relaxed and happy. "You are looking well, Daniel. I love seeing you so happy. Has Alison got something to do with your relaxed manner? I must say—"

"Mom, stop!" Daniel interrupted. "You are prying and that's not like you."

Emma inhaled deeply. "I have so much catching up with you to do and I don't know where to begin."

"Not just now, please, Mom. I'm driving and I'm sure an intense question and answer session will be distracting. I'll put on the radio and we can both catch up on what's in the hit parade in this fabulous country."

My son is avoiding my questions, she thought. *I feel a remoteness I haven't felt before. Somehow, coming back to the home country has made me very unsure of myself. I didn't expect that and I don't like it.*

To the strains of John Travolta and Olivia Newton-John singing "You're the One That I Want," Emma smiled wryly, thinking, *Am I the one that you want, BJ, or more to the point, are you the one I want?*

Nine

The intended week in the Lake District wasn't going well and mother and son were both confused, although neither spoke of it to the other. Emma loved being with her son, but she was strangely uncertain about her relationship with him and she warily attempted on numerous occasions to clarify the situation without success. On the third day, as they were walking around the pretty village of Hawkshead, she ventured to initiate a meaningful conversation, not for the first time since they arrived. "Shall we go into this little tearoom and have a typically British afternoon tea?" she asked as they approached Buttercup's Café adjacent to the Beatrix Potter souvenir shop. "It will give us a chance to talk."

"If you like," Daniel replied, his tone distinctly lacking interest. "I'm not really bothered what we do."

"We don't have to if you think afternoon tea is for dowager ladies," Emma said, not hiding her rising irritation.

Daniel was taken aback. "My goodness, Mom. Don't put words into my mouth. I can think and speak for myself. What is the matter with you? I don't think I have ever seen you like this."

"Like what?" Emma snapped.

Daniel thought carefully before he spoke. "Well, it's difficult to put into words, but since degree day, you've been a bit preoccupied and when you speak, you either sound completely disinterested, or you ask questions that sound like you are probing for some sort of underhand information. I didn't even think about dowager ladies, but you seem to be answering your own question, if that's what you really think."

Emma looked at him and was forced to accept her little boy had suddenly, in her eyes, become a man whom she was having difficulty understanding. She felt her hackles rising and took a deep breath before she voiced her opinion. "My, my, Daniel, I don't think I'm different at all, but *you* have become a different person in my absence, haven't you?"

"What do you mean?" Daniel asked, uncertain where this conversation was heading.

"I mean, you are certainly not the person I saw last Christmas—the young man...the student who was still my loving son, the boy who shared everything with me and was always an open book as regards his ambitions and..." *How can I tell him how I feel when I don't know myself?*

"Hold on, Mom," Daniel interrupted. "This is what I have just been talking about. You appear to be stressed about something and I find myself almost waiting for the *Danny boy* eponym to be assigned to me. That in itself doesn't fill me with confidence."

Emma breathed in deeply. "Let's go back to the hotel and have afternoon tea there," she said. "We can have room service and then we'll be able to talk privately. I suspect the topic of the coming conversation is not for public airing."

"Whatever you prefer. I don't mind," Daniel answered compliantly.

They drove back to the Ashleigh Hotel in silence, neither wishing to break into the thoughts of the other.

~ * ~

"Now, where do we start, Daniel?" Emma asked tentatively.

"Where do you want to start?" he answered with a slight shrug.

"That's your father to a tee," Emma told him lightly.

"What is?"

"Shrugging when he's not quite sure how to answer a question," she explained. "He usually looks down at his shoes to hide his uneasiness. He did it when I first met him and he did it in the conference hall at the university when he wasn't certain how I would react as he arrived. He did it again on Sunday when he was clearly confused with my attitude towards him when we went to his house." She paused and looked at Daniel with eyes that showed the uncertainty she was feeling inside. "Do you mind listening for a little while? There are things I need to say in order to allow this conversation to go in the right direction."

Daniel nodded and made himself comfortable on the sofa while his mother sat upright in the armchair to his left, displaying a businesslike position as opposed to Daniel's casualness.

Taking in a deep breath, Emma began. "I feel lost, and I know that in itself will appear strange to you. I've never been uncertain in anything I do. I always pride myself that I have a clear outlook on life and my ambitions for you, whether they be guiding you as a little boy towards which game to play, or supporting your teenage trends and agreeing with your choice of subjects to study at university—"

"I know all that, Mom—"

"Please don't interrupt, Danny b..." She paused before she said what Daniel had predicted outside the tearoom in Hawkshead. "...bear with me, please, Daniel." She coughed nervously. "When BJ appeared at the degree ceremony, I was shocked and I must say, I was also angry inside. I initially felt he had no right to be there. In my head, I went through all the heartache he caused, but I gradually convinced myself that, of course he had a right to be there. He is your father, after all. After the shock, I remembered the love we shared, and when I gathered the courage to steal a look at him, I realised he was as confused as I was. Having said that, his confusion was probably not rising from the same source as mine, and I must confess, deep, deep down inside, I experienced something that suggested I might still love him...at least I think I might, even after so long. I felt a little of the nervous excitement I used to feel every time I saw him."

"So why all this cloak and dagger stuff?"

"No cloak and dagger stuff," she told him. "In the restaurant, when you, Alison and BJ were talking, I realised I'm not a part of your life here in this country and BJ is. I left England behind all those years ago and somewhere along the line, I have rejected my roots. I have forgotten what it means to be English. At lunch, I felt very alone, even though you were all there by my side. I'm scared, Daniel."

"Scared? What of?"

Emma blinked rapidly, trying to stop tears from falling. "I'm scared I don't belong here anymore, scared that what you have with BJ will replace what you have—had—with me, scared that Alison has got your love and you don't need mine anymore, scared that your life now will not include me, not need me in it. It is all so overwhelming and I feel as though I'm trapped somewhere between what was and what is. I have no idea where I fit in and the envy I am feeling, jealousy even, is clouding my judgment."

Daniel shifted uncomfortably in his seat. He thought carefully before he spoke. "It's difficult to know what to say. I am listening to what you are saying, but the words aren't coming from the woman I know as my mother. You're different, and I don't know why. I thought bringing BJ back into your life would make us into a family—something I haven't experienced before—"

Emma sighed loudly. "And I understand that totally, I do, but—"

"But what?" Daniel interrupted, irritated with his mother's assessment of what he had hoped would be a straightforward adjustment in their lives. "I didn't think there would be any problems."

"I somehow think you and BJ are wearing rose-coloured spectacles and I'm not. I've spent the past twenty odd years showing you that I can cope on my own, that *we* can cope without a father figure and I thought," she paused, "no, I *know* it worked."

"But that was then. This is now and we have the opportunity to begin again, to be a family like other families."

Emma shook her head slowly, trying to unscramble her brain. "Okay, I understand that, too, but we live in Jamaica and we have our surrogate family there, a family who has always been there to share our lives, ups and downs, highs and lows, whatever came along."

"Are you telling me you don't want to start over with Dad?" Daniel asked bluntly.

"I don't know," she admitted. "I honestly don't know."

"I don't understand you, Mom," Daniel stated with undisguised irritation. "A few minutes ago, you said you still love him. Surely love is what makes you want to be together, what will re-establish itself in all its glory when you spend time in each other's company again."

Emma stood and as she began to pace the floor, she instantly recalled BJ doing just that when she had told him she was pregnant. Forcing herself to return to her chair, she said quietly, "I said I *might* love him, Daniel, and that puts a whole new slant on things." She looked at the floor and without looking up, she said, "Apart from all that, there's something I haven't told you..."

Ten

Jamaica, September 1970

Emma and Ann were excited as they made their way to the local cinema. "I can't wait to see this movie," Emma said. "I love, love, love Clint Eastwood and to get to see the movie as soon as it comes out is such a treat."

"It sure is," Ann said. "I could fall in love with him, too, but I don't think Earl would like it."

They both giggled like school girls. "Is he married?" Emma asked seriously.

"Earl?" Ann asked, keeping up the school girl silliness. "'Course he is! He's married to me, but if you're talking about Clint Eastwood, I don't know. You might be in with a chance, Em. Shall I ask him when I see him?"

They both laughed raucously and then, as they took in deep breaths to stop their hilarity, Emma said seriously, "I'm available as always. I doubt if I will ever meet another man of my dreams..." She paused, sighed and then said wistfully, "Thanks, BJ. You stitched me up good and proper."

"I always said there was somebody out there for you, Em," Ann reminded her. "I still think that. Surely there isn't just one man in the whole world you might fall in love with."

"But I always compare them with *that* one," Emma admitted. "Not so much the looks, nor the personality, but the feeling I got every time I saw BJ and the butterflies that were always in my stomach just thinking about him. The guys I've dated occasionally do nothing for me in the whole scheme of things. They've been pleasant company, but none of them have had me floating on cloud nine again like I did with BJ." She looked at Ann and grinned. "Not that I've felt the need to allow them the opportunity on that score."

"Don't lose hope, Em," Ann encouraged. "You're still young enough to start over. For the record, have you told Daniel you're dating again?"

"God, no!" Emma exclaimed. "I don't think he'd understand and I don't want to bother him while he's away studying. Apart from that, all my dates have been one-offs. So far, I haven't even allowed goodnight kisses. I'm looking for that feeling, you know, the feeling you get when you really want or need to feel close to somebody." She paused and took hold of Ann's arm. "I'd hate anybody to think I'm stand-offish, though." She shrugged and instantly thought of BJ again.

"Okay," Ann agreed. "I'll let Earl and Leroy know they mustn't say anything over Christmas when Daniel is home from uni. Glory and Teddy are too full of what's going on in their own lives to be interested in anything else. I don't think they even know about your dates, not that we'd discuss *you* with them anyway."

Emma smiled at Ann. "Thanks, Ann. You're a great friend."

~ * ~

After the movie, they were leaving the cinema when Emma felt a tap on her shoulder. Thinking somebody was touching her unnecessarily, she turned quickly, ready to give a piece of her mind to her supposed offender.

"Hi, Emma," he said. "You *are* Emma, aren't you?"

Emma stared at the guy who appeared to recognise her. She screwed up her eyes in puzzlement and then smiled as she asked in astonishment, "Wayne?"

"Yeah! You remember? Hammersmith Palais, November, nineteen-forty."

Emma gasped and covered her mouth with her hand. "I do remember. How could I forget? You were there when the bombs dropped on my home. I never did get the chance to say thank you for that night, so thanks. You were a great help to me."

Ann looked from one to the other and then, while Emma recovered from the shock, she introduced herself. "Hi. I'm Ann, Emma's best friend. Nice to meet you, Wayne."

Wayne shook her hand and introduced his buddy. "This is Chas. We were in the RCAF together. He and his lovely wife, Mimi, are looking after me for a couple of weeks."

Pleasantries were shared all round and then Wayne said to Emma, "Would you and Ann like to come for a drink with us? It would be great to catch up."

Both Emma and Ann looked uncertain, but Wayne, realising their plight, added, "No strings attached. Just a drink and a chat." He laughed. "We're not trying to pick you up like we did during the war. Those days are long gone."

Emma looked at Ann for reassurance. "What do you think, Ann?" she asked. "It really would be great to catch up. Such a lot has happened in the past thirty years. I'm not sure one drink will give us enough time, but it will be a good start."

They found a cosy little bar just a few yards away from the cinema, and Wayne and Chas went to buy the drinks while Emma and Ann found a table. As they sat down, Ann looked at Emma and winked. "This is a turn up, isn't it? Is he the one you told me about on the way out here?"

"My lord, Ann! What a memory you have," Emma replied. "I'd forgotten all about that myself, but now you've said it, yes, he's the one."

"The one you said you might have taken further if you'd had the chance?"

"Hey, hold on a bit!" Emma interrupted. "He's probably married with lots of kids. Don't go down that road, Mrs Brown."

Wayne and Chas returned to join the ladies and placed the drinks on the table. "Sitting at the table is much better than crouching under it," Wayne joked. "I think the last time I sat with you, Emma, we were under a table sheltering from the bombs."

"Yes, we were," Emma agreed. "I don't think I want to go through those times ever again."

"Me neither," Ann said. "I did that a few times, too, but usually in a pub on the Old Kent Road. That's how I met Earl...my husband," she added, to make sure the two guys had that snippet of information.

"That must be uncommon," Chas said. "I guess there's a story in there somewhere."

"Indeed there is, "Ann told him. "A trip across an ocean in the middle of a war, a shotgun wedding, two children, and twenty-seven years later, they all lived happily ever after."

"Wow!" Wayne rejoined. "And what about you, Emma? Do you have a story to tell?"

Emma smiled. "No, not really," she told him. "A lot has happened in the past thirty years as I said before, but suffice to say, I'm here and I survived." She decided on the spot that her thoughts were best kept to herself. *I'm not going to bare my soul to you just now, Wayne. It's good to see you, but you don't need to know every detail of my life.*

Wayne astutely observed the quiet demeanour accompanying Emma's answer and instantly made the conversation about himself. "Well, after I left you in London, Emma, I was ordered to Coastal Command and I helped sink a few German U-boats in the North Sea. I didn't go home until early 1946 and was de-mobbed soon after I arrived in Vancouver."

The conversation was easy, not so much reminiscing, but more about worldly topics: weather, cricket, movies, anything that wasn't too personal. By ten-thirty, they had put the world to rights and Ann suggested they leave before they were thrown out. "Closing time," she announced.

Automatically, they all looked at their watches. "There's still time for another drink," Chas suggested.

"For you, maybe, but not for us," Emma said. "We're working tomorrow, so it's time we went home."

"Can I walk you home?" Wayne asked. "I promise there'll be no bombs tonight."

"Ha-ha, very funny," Emma scoffed light-heartedly. "I'm driving and I'll drop Ann off on the way. Do you need a ride?"

"No thanks," Wayne answered. "Chas lives just a few blocks from here. I'm here for the rest of the week and Chas has to earn a living to feed his family, so I'm left to my own devices most of the time, but I'd like to see you again, Emma. May I have your number so we can catch up some more?"

Emma looked at Ann. "I *would* like to catch up some more."

Ann grinned.

Taking Ann's expression as the encouragement she needed, she scribbled her number on a coaster. "I work nine till three most days, so please don't phone until about three-thirty or four o'clock."

~ * ~

In the car on the way home, Ann couldn't resist asking Emma the question. "Do you think this might go somewhere?"

"What do you mean, *go somewhere*?"

"Well, he didn't mention a wife and kids back home in Vancouver, did he?" Ann asked, not waiting for an answer. "He was certainly eager to see you again."

"Ann!" Emma chastised. "Why are you so keen to get me hooked up to somebody? I'm all right as I am."

"No, you're not, Em," Ann retaliated. "Before we went into the cinema, you were wondering if you might meet your Mr Right one day. That proves you think about it and I'll bet it crosses your mind every time you're with Earl and me and with Cherelle and Leroy. I have often thought you might feel lonely at those times."

Emma pondered for a little while before she answered. "You know," she said, "I do sometimes feel like a spare part, even though you all make me feel wanted. It takes all my resolve at times not to burst into tears because you are all so happy together and I'm on my own. I'm the odd one out."

"Is that why you occasionally refuse our invitations to join us when we decide to go to the Mexicana for dinner?"

Emma grimaced. "If I'm honest, yes, it is," she admitted. "You are all my friends and I know you wouldn't deliberately make me feel uncomfortable, but sometimes I do. I imagine people staring and wondering why I haven't got a partner when you and Cherelle have."

"That's silly, Em, and you know it."

"Maybe it is, but I'm almost forty-nine years old and it's difficult not to come across as somebody who's been left on the shelf, or somebody whose reputation is that of being a frustrated old maid."

"Lordy, lordy, Emma," Ann chimed in. "We are feeling sorry for ourselves tonight, aren't we? Forty-nine, or twenty-nine, you are still very attractive and there must be lots of men who would like to be with you. As far as I can see, Wayne thinks that, too."

"Come on, Ann, my dear friend. It's thirty years since I saw Wayne and then it was only for a very brief time. He was nice then and he seems as though he's nice now, but I wouldn't be looking to fall in love with him just because we met previously. Anyway, he's bound to be married, so end of story. Guys like him are never left on the shelf, more's the pity. Give it a rest...please, Ann." Emma was irritated with her friend and that didn't happen very often, if at all.

Ann knew she had overstepped the mark. "Sorry, Em," she said sheepishly. "I just want you to meet somebody to love and who would love you in return. I won't push it any further, but you will see him again, won't you?"

Eleven

The following day, Wayne called at precisely three-thirty just as Emma was walking through the door of her home. "Wow, that's good timing," she said cheerily. "I just walked in. How are you today?"

"I'm good, thanks," Wayne said. "And you?"

"Yes, I'm fine. Pleased to be home from work and, although I do love my job, it's always nice to be home afterwards."

Wayne got straight to the point. "When can I see you, Emma?"

"When would you like to see me?"

"Now?"

"Wow, why are you in such a hurry?".

"Please don't take this the wrong way, but I need to talk to you and I would like to do it face to face," he said earnestly.

Emma was puzzled. "My, my," she said, so as to gain a few more seconds to think what to say in reply. "It sounds urgent and I can't for the life of me think what it might be unless you have decided to fly home to your wife and family tonight."

"No, not that, but it might loosely have something to do with it."

"Oh," Emma replied. "Curiouser and curiouser, as Alice in Wonderland said." Her thoughts confirmed what she had suggested to Ann the night before. *So he is married, after all. I hope it's not a 'my wife doesn't understand me' situation.*

"Well?" Wayne asked, urgency showing in his tone.

Emma thought for a moment. "Would it be too forward of me to invite you here for dinner? I have only just walked in from work and dinner won't be sumptuous, but it will be edible and nutritious."

"That would be great, if you don't mind cooking for two...it is for two, isn't it? Ann did mention you lived alone."

Emma sighed, not resignedly, but more out of wanting to get to the bottom of what Wayne was avoiding saying on the phone. "Come round anytime," she said. "You'll have to take pot luck with dinner."

"I'll be there in a few minutes," he said. "I took the liberty of looking in the phone directory to find your address. I'm in the public phone kiosk just down the road." With that, he put the phone down and before Emma had removed her jacket, he was at the door.

Emma couldn't hide her puzzlement as she opened her door to the person who, thirty years before, had held her hand as she desperately searched the rubble to find her mother. *Allowing him into my home might suggest something to him and I'm certainly not up for anything but a chat. How could I think anything else when talking to a married man? I don't even know why I'm thinking these things. Get a grip, Em.* Deciding to be open and honest from the start, she said quietly, "I have to say, Wayne, I have no idea what you're up to and I'm feeling decidedly unnerved by the urgency in your tone. What's going on here?"

Wayne was quick to answer. "Please don't be concerned," he said. "I want you to understand my situation, that's all. Seeing you last night after thirty years was something I never even dreamed of—"

"Why would you?" Emma interrupted. "Why would you even think about us?" *Oh, my lord! Did I say 'us'?* "I mean," she said quickly to cover her *faux pas*, "I mean we didn't know each other...we just danced together a couple of times."

"And what a great dancer you were," he recalled. "I haven't forgotten that."

Emma smiled. "So what's all this about?"

"Can we sit?" Wayne asked. "I need to tell you something."

Emma led him into the sitting room and offered him a seat on the sofa. She sat on the adjacent armchair and deliberately made herself comfortable, at least to give the impression she was relaxed, when she was anything but.

Wayne sat forward with his elbows on his knees and looked directly at Emma. "I know this is going to sound ridiculous," he said "but don't judge me until I've finished what I want to say."

Emma took a deep breath and, cocking her head to one side, she smiled in an effort to put them both at their ease. "Go ahead," she said. "I'm listening."

"First of all, I have to tell you I'm going through divorce. It's been a traumatic time for me and I'm not at fault. My wife...ex-wife, decided to take up with my best mate while I was working. I came home to find him in my bed."

Emma felt her heart sink for him. "That must have been terrible for you," she told him gently.

"It was, but looking back, I should have read the signs years ago. I was blind to what was going on under my nose," he explained. "Now, I'm fine and know I can face the world again.

Chas came to my rescue and has been there for me. He knew I needed to get away from the situation at home and invited me here. Comrades in arms never let you down."

Emma subconsciously leaned forward and took his hand.

Wayne willingly took her hand and enclosed it in both of his. "Last night when I saw you, I saw the happy, lively young girl I had met at the Hammersmith Palais all those years ago. My heart flipped and I instantly recalled the disappointment in being posted away from London and never seeing you again. I told you it would sound ridiculous, and I wouldn't blame you if you told me I'm on the rebound and looking for comfort from a woman, but please Emma, will you allow me to see you while I'm here? I have until the end of the week and then I have to be back in Vancouver. I need to make sure my lawyer has everything in place before I sign anything. It might take days, weeks, or months, but after that, I never have to have anything to do with her again."

Emma was dumbstruck. She looked at him, still allowing him to hold her hand, but she said nothing.

"Say something, please, Emma," he pleaded. "I need to know I'm not being too much of a fool wishing to make up for the time I wanted to spend with you in nineteen-forty. Please don't say I've missed the boat. You have appeared at a time when I need—"

Emma breathed in deeply again. "You know," she interrupted in almost a whisper. "I am the most sensible and logical woman on this earth..." She paused, allowing herself to make what was turning out to be a very illogical decision. "...but I *would* like to see you again. I never make spur of the moment decisions and I can't believe I am so open to allowing you into my world to see wherever it might take us. I don't really know you and there is a lot you don't know about me, but we don't need to know any of it just now. I'm single, and to all intents and purposes, you are, or will be single too, so I'm willing to try, Mr...I don't even know your surname!"

They laughed out loud, stood and hugged warmly. "My full name is Wayne Louis Robards. My great-great grandparents migrated from France to Toronto in the late eighteen hundreds. My family travelled to the west coast of Canada just before the last war. They set up a wine merchants' business in Vancouver and we have lived there ever since. I have an older sister and a younger brother, both married with grown children."

"Do you have children?" Emma asked.

"No," he said sadly. "It just never happened, but at least being childless has made divorce easier."

"I guess," Emma agreed. "I have a son, Daniel. He's studying in England. There's a long story there, but I'll tell you about that later. No need to go into detail at this point. Now, I think we should eat.

~ * ~

For the rest of the week, five days in all, Wayne was waiting for her each day as she finished work. They went out for dinner each evening and went to Emma's house for drinks afterwards. They hugged each other as he left her house each night, nothing more. Their last day together was Saturday and Emma suggested they pack a picnic lunch and go to Wickie Wackie Beach. "With a name like that, you have to see it for yourself," she told him. "The ocean is pretty wild out there and surfers love it, yet, strange though it may seem, it is also very peaceful if we can find a sheltered spot."

"Sounds good," Wayne said. "Will you drive, or shall I?"

"You drive," Emma suggested. "I'll pack the picnic basket and make sure we have sodas to drink, unless you think I should take a thermos?"

Wayne shook his head. "Sodas will be fine. We can always buy coffees if we need a warm drink."

"So late in September, the beach shouldn't be too busy, but the weather is still warm enough to be pleasant for us to have a picnic," she told him.

They wandered along the beach for a while, hand in hand like two teenagers. Intermittently, they smiled at each other and Wayne occasionally shook his head slowly in disbelief. They sat on the beach mat and ate jerk chicken sandwiches and potato chips, then drank their orange sodas.

"I can't believe so much has happened in so few days," he announced. "This time last week, I was pouring my heart out to Chas and Mimi about how fed up I was. That was when Chas suggested we go to the movies to allow me to get lost in a fantasy world for a while. Do you think Fate took a hand in our meeting?"

"Maybe," Emma told him. "I do believe in Fate, but it doesn't always work in your favour."

"What do you mean?"

In her explanation, Emma briefly related her fateful meeting with the man with whom she had fallen deeply in love without mentioning his name, and even more briefly still, how she returned to Jamaica to have her baby. "Probably just as fateful before that was my meeting of Merle Thomson in nineteen forty-three when I first arrived here. I became her housekeeper and companion. She left me her house in her will, hence, that's why I'm here now."

"Wow! That was some twist of Fate in your favour, Emma," Wayne said. "Have you never been back to Blighty since having your son?"

"No, I haven't," she admitted. "My life is here and..." She stopped as she silently recalled the bitterness of her aunt and the lack of complete recognition from her father. "I really have nothing to return for," she said sadly.

"But Daniel is there now, isn't he?"

"Yes, but he'll be home for Christmas, so I have that to look forward to." She began to gather up what was left of their picnic lunch. "Shall we wander round the town and find a bakery for dessert?"

"Sounds good to me," Wayne agreed. "I insist I buy whatever you desire. For my part, I just love Jamaican rum cake—"

"Cupcakes for me," Emma interrupted. "Any flavour with lots of butter cream on top."

"Your wish is my command, lovely lady. Thank you for the delicious picnic food. I could really get used to this."

~ * ~

Back at her house, she made afternoon tea and they sat in the garden listening to Emma's record collection. "Not exactly the hits of today, but a lot of my records belonged to Merle, and even the scratchy ones bring back fond memories."

"Do you have any swing?" Wayne asked. "We could dance again like we did at the Hammersmith Palais. We could see if we still make a good couple."

"Actually, I do have a few," Emma said laughing. "I have 'Chattanooga Choo- Choo' and 'Boogie Woogie Bugle Boy.' I bet they would help us re-live those times."

She went inside through the French doors that were wide open to allow the music to be heard in the garden. She put the phonograph on and Wayne stood as she returned. "Beautiful lady, may I have this dance?"

Emma laughed. "*Déjà vu!*" She kicked off her shoes and they turned back the clock as they once again complemented each other's snappy foot movements and coordinated twists and turns in perfect unison.

"We've still got it," Wayne said as the music came to an end. "I think I said we were made for each other that night at the Palais..."

Emma stopped abruptly, took Wayne's face in her hands and drew him close. As their lips met, she found herself enfolded in his arms and felt the beating of his heart, a moment of joy, a moment of abandonment, a moment of intimacy.

"Oh, Emma," he breathed hoarsely as he nuzzled her hair.

Suddenly, she broke away and turned her back on him, covering her face with her hands.

Wayne was surprised at her withdrawal from his embrace. "Emma, what is it? What's wrong?"

Emma turned to face him again, her eyes brimming with tears. "Nothing wrong," she told him. "These are happy tears."

Wayne sighed with relief. "I thought I had done something to upset you."

Regaining her composure, Emma took his hand and led him to where they had been sitting before they had begun to dance. Keeping hold of his hand, she looked into his eyes and said, "You are the first man I have allowed to kiss me like that since Daniel's father. I never expected I would experience those intimate feelings with anybody else. Just then, I felt the longing and the passion I felt with BJ. You unlocked feelings I have guarded with my life since I left England all those years ago."

"That can only be good, can't it?" Wayne suggested.

"I guess so, but you are leaving tomorrow and I don't want to..."

"Don't want to what?"

Emma looked lovingly into his eyes, eyes that were gleaming with the love and affection she hadn't seen since she had first kissed BJ. "It took me by surprise, Wayne, and I don't want to take this further just now. You are going back to Vancouver and I don't know when I'll see you again, or *if* I will ever see you again."

Wayne knelt in front of her and took both her hands in his. "I have to go home, and it's true, I don't know when I'll be back..."

"And Christmas is coming when Daniel will be home."

"I understand, Emma," Wayne assured her. "We have only just reconnected, and with my situation and everything it involves, we need to take our time. However, you needn't worry that I won't be back. It might be a good idea if we stay in touch by phone and letter if you like, but I'll come back after Christmas and see how we go then."

"That sounds good to me," she replied. "We have definitely discovered something very strong between us and I don't want to dismiss it without seeing where it leads."

"It sounds so clinical, put like that," he commented. "I think it's love. I know it's love and it deserves to be allowed to grow."

Emma smiled warmly. "Okay," she said. "Exciting, isn't it?"

With that Wayne took her in his arms again and kissed her gently—nothing urgent about it, just lovingly and warmly, a kiss full of love and affection and...dare he think it? *Full of romantic promise.*

Still holding her close, he asked, "Who's BJ?"

Emma was stunned. "Did I mention BJ?" she asked, without hiding her surprise.

"You did," Wayne told her kindly.

Emma sighed. "He's Daniel's father and he's BJ Johnson, the writer and social commentator. I doubt you've ever heard of him, but my friend in England tells me he's becoming quite well known."

"Oh, wow!" Wayne exclaimed. "I love his work."

"You mean you've heard of him in Canada? Blimey!" She paused. "Please don't ask me to discuss his books, because I have deliberately not read them," she said amicably. "I simply don't want him to affect my life any more than he has already. I don't mention him at all to Daniel now. There's no point. Daniel's old enough to realise BJ doesn't feature in our lives...never did, never will."

"But didn't you say Daniel is at university in England?" Wayne asked. "Doesn't that pose a threat?"

"Not really," Emma confirmed. "He's in his final year now and it's highly unlikely he'll just bump into BJ on the street. I know he reads his books in the course of his studies, especially since he is doing a social sciences and politics degree, but I'm not worried about that. Daniel is very level-headed and I'm sure he'll just get on with his work as required. He seems happy there and I am so looking forward to seeing him at Christmas." She paused again and then said firmly, "I won't tell him about you, though. After all, *we* don't know where it's leading, so it will be best to leave well alone as far as Daniel's concerned."

"Point taken," Wayne replied. "I understand."

Before he left, they kissed again and bid their fond farewells. "I'll call you as soon as I land. Take care, Emma. I'll miss you."

She smiled and hugged him affectionately. "I'll miss you, too. Safe journey."

Twelve

In Emma's room at The Midland, Daniel stared at his mother with complete shock. "You have never kept secrets from me, Mom, except when it involved what Santa was going to bring me each Christmas when I was a little boy."

Emma smiled. "That was a lovely time. I just adored seeing your little face light up when you opened your presents. I miss those times."

"So what haven't you told me?" he asked, before his mother could take off on a flight of fanciful memories about his childhood.

"Oh yes, that," she said, her expression a cross between apprehension and guilt. "Promise me you won't go mad when all is revealed."

"Oh my! That sounds ominous. How can I promise how I'm going to react when I have no idea what you're going to tell me?"

"It's going to take a while for me to put you up to speed, so bear with me," Emma told him and she breathed in deeply before she continued quietly, "...during the war, when I was still very young and in London, I used to go out dancing at the Hammersmith Palais..."

Emma quietly reminisced about what had happened in London in 1940 and related to Daniel the night she had met a Canadian gunner named Wayne.

"May I have this dance, beautiful lady?"

"He was a handsome guy and his accent was really attractive to me. He was such a good dancer, too." She smiled as her mind wandered back to that fateful night at the Palais.

Emma had beamed. "How could I refuse such a lovely request?" He took her hand and led her to the middle of the dance floor as her friend, Mavis, got up to dance with his mate.

The boogie-woogie beat had them tapping their feet and swing dancing with happy abandon. "Gee, you sure can dance, miss," he complimented.

Emma grinned. "Only when I have a good partner," she replied, between twists and turns and snappy foot movements that completely complemented those of her partner.

"We should do this more often," he said. "I have never had a girl dance with me so well. We were made for each other."

Emma laughed out loud. "I bet you say that to all the girls, you smooth talker. I've heard all about you GIs. What's your name?"

"I'm Wayne, and you might have heard about GIs, but I'm Canadian, not American and I'm not in the army. I'm in the RCAF and a rear gunner. I'm in London because I have a few days' leave. I need to go back to the base in North Yorkshire the day after tomorrow, but like I said before, you really are a good dancer." He laughed with her as the honky-tonk music came to an end.

"But what's Hammersmith Palais got to do with keeping something from me?" Daniel asked. "It was all such a long time ago."

"I'll get to it in a minute," Emma replied. "A couple of months before you came home for Christmas last year, Auntie Ann and I went to the movies to see *Kelly's Heroes*, because we were both so in love with Clint Eastwood, and as you know, it's rare for our little cinema to show such an up-to-date movie. As we were coming out after the show, I felt a tap on my shoulder…"

"And?"

"Well, it was Wayne, the Canadian guy I had danced with all those years ago. Can you believe it?"

"It does take a bit of believing. What was he doing in Kingston?"

"He told me he was visiting one of his buddies from his days in the Royal Canadian Air Force. He was absolutely shocked to see me there. He had no idea I had migrated, well, how could he? The last I saw of him was the night the bombs landed on our house…the night my mum died. He was so kind and caring that night. He went back to his base in Yorkshire after that and I didn't see him again. I was surprised he recognised me after all that time."

"I'm getting confused, Mom. What's he got to do with the mood you've been in since you got here, and why didn't you tell me about him when I was home for Christmas?" Daniel inquired. "I'd have thought you would have been very excited to tell me something like that."

Emma took a deep breath. "He asked me out."

"And?"

"I saw him every day until he flew home to Vancouver. We sort of…"

Daniel stood from the sofa, walked a few steps away from Emma and then turned to face her. "Are you telling me you and he…" He paused and stared at his mother in amazement. "Are you telling me you and he hit it off, got it on, or whatever you oldies call it?”

Emma pressed her lips together and looked at Daniel, a mixture of guilt, sorrow, irritation and confusion filling her mind. “Before you go off at the deep end, you need to consider that *you* had seen your father before you went home last year and you didn’t tell *me*. Had he not been at the degree ceremony, I would be none the wiser.”

“I would have told you eventually,” Daniel said, a hint of belligerence in his attitude. “I needed to get my head around it myself before I decided what to do. I thought telling you in advance would have created all sorts of issues for you and I didn’t want to be worrying about you while I was revising for my exams.”

“But it was all right for you to be meeting your father behind my back?”

“It wasn’t like that,” Daniel asserted.

“Well, what was it like, Danny boy?

Daniel returned to his seat moodily. “I had a right to meet my father...”

Emma gasped. “Just be careful, Daniel,” she said quietly. “Talking of rights might open a whole can of worms. Most rights come with accompanying wrongs, and at the risk of confusion and contradiction, I can think of many wrongs that don’t give a person any viable rights whatsoever. Think carefully before you lay down *your* rights.”

Daniel leaned forward, rested his elbows on his knees and held his head in his hands. Looking directly at his mother he said, “Just tell me straight, Mom. Did you sleep with the guy?”

“Whether I did or did not is really none of your business, but we spent a lot of time together and decided we might see where our reconnection takes us. I like him and he likes me.” She paused for a moment and inhaled deeply. “He’s married—well, separated—and that's part of the reason I didn't tell you about him. He's actually going through divorce..."

"Oh great," Daniel said disdainfully. "Now you'll be tarnished with *the other woman* label. What were you thinking, Mom?"

Emma was quick to reply. "No, I won't. He is divorcing his wife because of *her* infidelity. He caught her in bed with his best friend..."

"Some best friend then!"

"Wayne and I have kept in touch and will continue to do so until his divorce is finalised. He has been back for long weekends a few times since our first meeting. He mentioned something to Auntie Ann before he left last time, and you know how well Auntie Ann keeps secrets! He was talking about moving to Jamaica and making a fresh start..."

"With you?" Daniel asked.

"Who knows?" Emma said. "Meeting your father again has given me a lot to think about, hence my confusion and my feelings of uncertainty. The whole thing makes me feel as though I'm caught between a rock and a hard place. On the one hand, I remember the power of new love between BJ and the *younger* me, and on the other, Wayne makes me feel loved as I am *now*. We are experiencing mature love, even though I have been very cautious about allowing my feelings to run away with me. With BJ it was first love, first passion, but in spite of its intensity, it was a love we weren't ready to be open about. It was a secret affair, an affair neither of us knew how to deal with. Hence, I ran away to Jamaica, knowing I had understanding friends there who wouldn't judge me, or condemn me for falling in love with the wrong man, wrong that is, in the eyes of ignorant people. You know the rest."

Daniel stood and walked over to Emma, whose eyes had filled with unshed tears. He pulled her from her chair and enveloped her in the warmth of his embrace. "Oh lordy, lordy, Mom," he whispered. "Don't cry. Please forgive me for being judgmental. I don't want to admit this, but I am wondering whether or not I should have just presumed you and Dad would get back together. Even when I was very young, I thought you still loved Dad, because whenever you told me about him, you always had a dreamy look in your eyes. What right have I to say who you spend your life with? God knows, I would like nothing better for you, BJ and me to be a family, but I think I'm old enough to understand that first love can't always be forever love." He paused and slowly shook his head. "My first love was Cindy Wallace at high school, and I can't see me rekindling that...*ever*. I heard she married as soon as she left school and now has four children. Seems I had a lucky escape." He smiled as he remembered Cindy and her teenage reputation. *I thought I might discover my prowess as a lover at the tender age of sixteen.* "I want you and Dad to be together, I can't deny that, but not if you have doubts about giving yourself whole-heartedly to him as a wife and mother. I need a mom and dad who love each other. It's a selfish thought on my part, but..."

Emma held him at arms' length. "It isn't a selfish thought, but I can't give you a straight answer, Daniel. Please don't you worry about it," she told him. "What will be, will be, but I need to talk seriously with BJ at the weekend before I leave on Sunday night. I'm not sure I'll find the right words, but I'll have to try."

Thirteen

In Stratford upon Avon, BJ Johnson reflected on his own reaction when Emma had once again run away from a situation seemingly too difficult with which to deal. *I can't believe my thoughts went to Gracie when I selfishly needed reassuring just because my relationship with Emma is not as straightforward as I imagined it would be,* he silently reasoned. *I really have no idea what is going on in Emma's head, but my friendship with Gracie has suddenly become a bone of contention for me. I really shouldn't be trying to blame Gracie for my own confused feelings. She does, however, have a way of bringing me down to earth and I have to agree, we are good together. I like her very much, and at one time I might have considered taking it further, but I have never felt comfortable taking that massive step. Once Daniel appeared, my deep feelings for Emma re-surfaced and I know she was...is...the love of my life.* He rested his elbows on his desk and held his head in his hands. *Sort yourself out,* he silently told himself. *Enough of this procrastination.*

Suddenly his telephone rang and he ran to answer it. Recalling what he had done a couple of days before when he thought it might be Emma and it turned out to be Gracie, he answered with caution. "Hello? BJ Johnson."

"Hi, Dad."

"Daniel! Good to hear from you. How are you? When did you get back? Did you have a good time? How is your mom?"

"Slow down, Dad!" Daniel instructed. "You're going at a million miles an hour."

"Sorry," BJ said.

"Mom is back at The Midland. She said she'll call you tomorrow. I'll be off to Liverpool to catch up with Alison as soon as Mom is checked in at the airport on Sunday. We have a lot to sort out before the first week in September when Ali starts her new teaching post." Daniel felt guilty. *I haven't told either of my parents what my plans are. I need to get all my ducks in a row before I can share my future with them. Whether I tell them together, or separately, is up to Mom. She has a lot to sort out too, more emotional, I think, than physical stuff, but that's not my call to make and I don't want to give Dad any hint of what is going on in her world. Too complicated by half.* "I'll call you later once I know what is happening in Liverpool."

"Are you and Alison getting together?" BJ asked openly.

Daniel breathed in deeply. "I don't want to say anything until I've seen Ali. Please don't breathe a word of this to Mom when you see her. I haven't mentioned that I'm not going back to Jamaica and that might be quite a shock for her. I'm surprised she hasn't already bought me a ticket to fly home with her, but please, Dad. Not one word."

~ * ~

It was Saturday morning when Emma called BJ. "Hi," she said quietly.

"Hi back," BJ answered. "How are you?"

"Good, I think," she replied, the uncertainty she was still feeling inside apparent in her tone. "May I come to see you today?"

"Of course. Would you like me to come for you?"

"No...thank you. I'll get a cab," she told him. "I'll be there at two-thirty. Is that okay with you?"

"That's fine," he said. "I'll have the kettle on..." He paused poignantly. "Just like the old times, Emma."

Emma deliberately didn't reply immediately. *Don't keep harking back to the old times, BJ. I need to process my thoughts on what is happening now, not what happened all those years ago.* "I'll see you at two-thirty then. Bye."

With that, the phone went dead.

She arrived a few minutes after two-thirty and BJ opened the door to her as soon as the taxi drew up at his gate, so he was able to welcome her into his home again. "Hi, Emma," he called out cheerily. "So good to see you again. Come in! I have the kettle on. I think we'll sit in the lounge today. It's much more comfortable in there."

He's nervous, Emma thought. *He's gabbling. Oh Lord, please give me strength to find the right words.* "Thank you," she said. "Sounds good to me."

She made herself comfortable and waited for BJ to come in with a tea tray as he had done the week before. When he placed it on the coffee table, he looked up and asked if she would like him to pour.

"Yes, please. Milk, no sugar."

"I know that, Emma. You have no need to remind me."

She sat forward in her chair and reached for her cup and saucer, placing them gently on her lap and holding them so as not to spill anything on BJ's beige Wilton carpet. Watching him discreetly while he settled himself on the settee to her right, she took a sip of her tea to help moisten her dry throat. *This is silly,* she thought. *We are both behaving like apprehensive teenagers. Here goes.* "I leave tomorrow night, BJ, and there are things that must be discussed before I go back to Jamaica."

"Do you have to go back?" BJ blurted.

"I do, and may I ask you not to assume anything about what is happening between you and me?"

BJ leaned back in his seat and stared at Emma with questioning eyes. "I need to assume something, Emma, for sanity's sake. You surely know my love for you has not changed."

"Don't go down that road just yet, BJ," she instructed firmly. "It's over twenty years since we were together and it all ended so miserably. The only good thing to come out of it, is Daniel."

BJ was stunned. "I have cherished the memory of you for all those years, Emma, but you seem to be dismissing it as though you never cared."

"Oh, I cared, BJ, so, so much, but we parted on very bad terms and you have no idea how long I kept those feelings locked in my heart. Even now, I'm not sure how I feel about you. I still remember the endearing qualities that made my heart leap for years..."

"Then why is it a problem now?"

"I never thought I would see you again. I had begun to get you out of my system. I was trying to move on. When you arrived at the degree ceremony, I was shocked...more than shocked, if I'm honest. I hated you and loved you again all in the space of a few minutes and then I became totally confused."

"Why were you confused if you felt your love for me again?"

"Because I had no control over my feelings at that point, or so it seemed, and when I learned that Daniel had been seeing you behind my back, I felt isolated, like I wasn't a part of his life anymore. He has never kept anything from me in his life. I don't like the deceit that you and he have concocted between you."

BJ's voice betrayed his irritation. "Hold on there, Emma. We didn't concoct anything. It was Daniel's decision not to tell you, and he made that decision so you wouldn't worry about him—or me—or whatever during his exams. Anyway, I believe he told you he had read my books, so you should have realised he was taking an interest in me through my writing."

Emma sighed. "I did know that, but I didn't think it would lead to your meeting. I knew nothing of the lecture you gave at the university and I can't believe it had all happened before he went home for Christmas. That Christmas, we had the best time and he didn't breathe a word of your appearance in his life."

"What would you have done if he'd said he'd met me?" BJ asked pointedly.

"To be honest, I don't know," she admitted. "We have a wonderful life in Jamaica and an even more wonderful set of friends who have become our surrogate family. Daniel knows I wouldn't just leave them behind, nor all they mean to me. I owe them so much."

"What makes them better than a real family, Emma?"

"Do you really want me to tell you, BJ?" she answered. "It wouldn't be very complimentary to you."

"I see," he said, with a hint of sarcasm in his tone again. "What they know of me from you has turned them against me even before they've met me. Are they all Black?"

Emma was stunned. "My god, BJ. Why would you ask that? You know my feelings on that score, but for your information, no, they aren't."

"Are any of them Black?"

"Stop this, BJ. Have you learned nothing in the past twenty-odd years?"

"I need to know, Emma," he said. "I have spent the last twenty-three years as a Black man living in a community with a white majority. Living in Jamaica must be the complete opposite for you, so you must know how it feels."

"You amaze me, BJ, and yes, white faces are perhaps in a minority where I live, but attitudes have changed and I can honestly say I have never been hurt, nor hindered, by prejudice against me. You knew my opinion when we were together, but it wasn't enough for us to be openly honest about our relationship. Together, we made our decision to keep our relationship secret. Neither of us had the courage to be open about it. Surely you don't need to be reminded of that. Last week, when we were about to walk along the river, it seemed you still had concerns about being seen with me in public. I didn't understand that. I still don't, especially since you are apparently well known for your views on racial equality."

BJ looked down and sighed. "Why are we here, Emma?" he asked resignedly. "I thought we would be discussing the possibility of getting back together for Daniel's sake. We have both admitted there might be some feelings there on both our parts. Isn't that worth pursuing, starting over and seeing where it goes? Love like we had never really goes away, does it?"

"What are you saying, BJ? It can't be just for Daniel's sake. My feelings have changed. I'm older and I'm not looking for urgent, passion-filled consummation anymore," she told him. "We were much, much younger and our libidos got the better of us."

BJ looked aghast. "Are you saying making love means nothing to you anymore, Emma? I can't believe that, not of *you*."

"That's the whole point," she said with conviction. "It was my first sexual experience. It was wonderful, it was urgent, it was all-consuming, but then it all went wrong."

"But we're not old yet, Emma. We still have room for romance and love-making in our lives. Don't you think we might rekindle that desire?"

Suddenly there was loud knocking on the door and they both reacted by sitting bolt upright. BJ stood and said, "Whoever it is, I'll get rid of them. This is not the time for social gatherings. Excuse me, please." He left the room to see who was demanding his attention so urgently.

He opened the door slowly, but there was an almighty push from outside and Gracie forced her way in without invitation. "It's weekend, BJ," she said smiling. "I promise I won't fight. I just need your answer, for better or worse."

Fourteen

On that same Saturday afternoon, Daniel was considering his own situation. The timing of his mother's return to Jamaica couldn't have been worse. He needed more time to inform her of his plans. He called Alison to unload his dilemma on her. "You always look at problems logically and objectively," he said. "I'm in a quandary, Ali. I need you..."

"Aw, that's nice," she said. "I need you, too. I have missed you so much and I can't wait to see you tomorrow."

"That's part of the problem."

"It is?" Alison questioned, disbelief in her tone. "Don't you want to see me?"

"Don't be silly," he told her. "Of course, I want to see you. I can't wait, but Mom doesn't leave until tomorrow evening. She has to be at the airport by four-thirty for her seven-thirty flight to

Heathrow and she has a short transfer time before she flies home to Kingston, so I won't be able to leave for Liverpool until then."

"Are you going to Heathrow with her?"

"No, but I'll need to wait until she's checked in at Birmingham Airport before I can leave. I'm not sure if Dad will be there."

"Where is she now?" Alison asked.

"She's with Dad, trying to sort out what is happening between them. I hope he isn't going to have his heart broken again. Good luck to him with that, and Mom doesn't know where her heart belongs, here, or in Jamaica. It isn't going to be easy for either of them. To add to all that, where are we going to live in Liverpool?"

"Don't worry about that," Alison reassured him. "I have everything sorted. Mum's sister in Southport knows somebody who owns student accommodation in Aigburth..."

"Where on earth is Aigburth?" Daniel asked.

"It's in Liverpool and not too far from Childwall where my school is," she said. "There are also frequent buses into the city centre where you will be working with the City Council."

"That's another thing," he admitted. "I haven't told her, or Dad, where I'll be working. Dad knows I'm staying in England, but I've sworn him to secrecy until I can tell Mom myself."

"Why haven't you told them?"

Daniel sighed, a long, deep sigh that seemed to come from his toes. "There have been things happening here you wouldn't believe," he informed her. "I'll fill you in when I see you, but suffice to say, I don't think Mom will be happy when I tell her I have already secured a job with Liverpool Social Services and I won't be going home. I wish I'd been up front from the beginning, but the situation with Mom and Dad hasn't gone as I anticipated. I decided she had enough to sort out without my adding to her stress."

"Why is she stressed?"

"Because she met somebody in Kingston and she is more than confused who she loves most."

"Oh, my word!"

"So there you are, Ali, my love. It hasn't been plain sailing since you left Kendal just over a week ago."

Alison was momentarily quiet, but then she said, "It's difficult to understand why you haven't already discussed your future with both of them, Dan. I can't believe your job situation has never been on the agenda. That's the first thing my parents asked me when I qualified. What have you been talking about all week?"

"Mom has changed. She seems to be concerned with what is happening in her own life, not mine, and that's very unusual," Daniel revealed. "We didn't have a meaningful conversation until she told me about this Canadian guy. I can't quite put my finger on it, but she's different."

"Different how?"

"She isn't the fun-loving, super-understanding person she has always been throughout my life. She's gone all serious and moody. Each time I found an opening to tell her my plans, she changed the subject. She seemed to be prying and fishing for information and yet she didn't really give me a chance to tell her about anything. Eventually, I just switched off. It's difficult to explain. You'd have to be there to understand what I mean."

"Oh, Daniel! You are being so blind," Alison told him bluntly. "You haven't been honest with her, and I bet she sensed it. Surely you can understand that mums know these things. They possess ESP or something. She has probably seen a big difference in you and has been uncomfortable knowing you are keeping things from her," Alison told him. "Add to that, unexpectedly coming face to face with your dad. You should try to understand her position. I thought she was a bit tense when we were at lunch on degree day, didn't you? She didn't contribute much to the conversation."

"To be honest, I didn't notice. I was so thrilled about us all being together as a family for the first time in my life, but when we were in The Lakes, it was as though she didn't know how to start a conversation and that's not Mom at all. Maybe you're right about her sensing my reticence. You are so brilliant, Ali," he said lovingly. "What would I do without you?"

"I think you'd cope, but I'm glad to know you love me."

He paused and then continued, "I love you and I can't wait to see you tomorrow, and much as I would like to talk to you all day, I'd better go and finish packing my cases. Thanks for allowing me to unload."

"We're a team," Alison told him. "See you tomorrow night. Bye."

~ * ~

Back in Stratford Upon Avon, BJ caught hold of Gracie's arm before she forced her way into the sitting room. "This isn't a good time," he said quietly, yet firmly. "I hate to turn you away, but..."

Gracie wrenched her arm free. "It will never be a good time, if it were left to you, BJ." She walked confidently into the room where moments earlier, BJ had been endeavouring to coax Emma into rekindling their romance. Pushing the door wide open, Gracie stopped in her tracks. "Oh," she uttered, then sarcastically, "Sorry to intrude." She turned and looked pointedly first at BJ and then back at Emma.

Emma stood and was about to introduce herself to the woman in front of her whose expression clearly conveyed her confusion, when BJ jumped in. "Emma, this is my friend, Gracie. Gracie—Emma."

The two politely shook hands and then without ceremony, Gracie smiled. "Oh, now I understand."

"Understand what?" BJ asked forcefully.

Gracie continued undaunted, and trying to establish her position in BJ's life, she said, "I hope BJ has been looking after you properly. He did tell me about his friend from Jamaica, but I didn't know you were coming this afternoon. I would have prepared afternoon tea for you both."

"Gracie!" he snapped. "What are you talking about? Enough!"

Emma picked up her handbag and made to leave. BJ grabbed her arm in a similar manner he had tried to prevent Gracie from entering the house a few moments before. "Don't go, Emma," he pleaded. "We have so much to discuss before you leave the country tomorrow."

Emma smiled first at Gracie and then in BJ's direction. "I see you have everything you need here, BJ. No need for me to gatecrash the party. Nice to meet you, Gracie, and good to see you again, BJ. We'll catch up again—maybe a phone call, or a letter?"

"I'll give you a ride back to the hotel. It will take ages for a cab to get here," he suggested.

"I'll come too," Gracie butted in.

"Sorry, Gracie, not this time," BJ told her firmly. "I have some things I need to discuss with Emma about private business in Jamaica." *I hope Emma doesn't judge me too badly for telling a little white lie,* he thought and he looked to see if he might detect disapproval in her manner.

Gracie, however, was deflated and it showed. "Don't think you'll get rid of me that easily. I'll be waiting for you when you get back, BJ. Please don't be too long." Her words were clear but not antagonistic.

"As you please," BJ said amicably. "Come, Emma. Your carriage awaits."

The silence in the car was deafening. BJ gripped the steering wheel, tight knuckles displaying his tension as he drove. Emma was first to break the silence. "Pull over, BJ, before we veer off the road, and into a tree."

BJ obeyed, switched off the engine, and forced himself to physically relax. His mind, however, was in turmoil. *I didn't want to explain about Gracie. She—*

Emma interrupted his thoughts. "So you have yourself a beautiful woman, BJ. I'm pleased for you. Gracie is so much more your type..."

"That's sarcastic, Emma, and you know it," he scolded. "And to cut to the chase, I'm not in love with her...it's *you* I love."

"Does she know that?"

"She knows I'm not in love with her, but she knows nothing about you. I have always kept my connection with you and Daniel to myself and I have never led her to believe I love her."

"How callous are you, BJ?" Emma asked. "She is so obviously in love with you. I could see it in her eyes, in spite of her trying to be angry with you. Why would you want me to come between you and her?" Her thoughts were in overdrive. *If I mention Wayne, it will look like tit for tat and I wouldn't sully our relationships like that, mine nor BJ's.*

BJ breathed in deeply, swivelled in his seat to face Emma and looked into her eyes. "Gracie is a wonderful person and a very close friend. She would like to take our relationship further, but I have always been honest with her about how I feel. Even though it seems callous to you, until now Gracie has always said she likes the easy-come, easy-go arrangement. It's almost as if she's psychic in that she has never previously really pushed the permanence button. I think she senses there is somebody else, although she didn't know of your existence until I answered the phone and called her Emma. That's when she began to question my feelings for her. I know it must appear too convenient for me to say, but I have kept my love for you in my heart since the day you walked out of my flat in Slough. I regretted my actions then and I still regret how I treated you. I went to look for you, you know? I even went to Castle Mews..."

"Oh, I bet Auntie Edith would have loved that."

"Well, yes, but I weathered that storm and left Windsor to restart my journey in becoming a British citizen. It worked, but I still thought about you all the time. When I left teaching and started to write full time, I moved here and joined a Caribbean group which meets once a month for drinks and socialising. That's where I met Gracie. She's a nurse...she's intelligent and she's fun to be with."

"Do you sleep with her?" Emma asked calmly.

BJ looked surprised. "Do you really need to know that, Emma?"

"Yes, I do."

"Why?"

Emma thought before she spoke. "This may sound very naïve, but I still think making love is just *that*, showing that you love the person who is lying close to you, feeling hearts beating as one, enjoying the need for intimacy in all its worldly sensuousness."

"My god, Emma," BJ exclaimed laughing. "I'm the writer here..."

Emma stopped her explanation abruptly. "Sex is sacred to me, BJ."

BJ patted her knee. "Oh Emma, I'm not belittling you."

"Then what *are* you doing?" she asked, irritated by his apparent disregard for her feelings. "Patting my knee like that is patronising in the extreme."

BJ sighed deeply. "Sorry," he said quietly. "I didn't know you were..."

"That's just it, BJ," she retorted. "We don't know each other at all. When we went out to lunch, I realised I had never been in a restaurant with you; never been in a car with you, didn't even know you could drive, and most of all, I had never been seen in a public place with you. How can you even think about getting together again when we know so little about each other?"

"What about our feelings?" BJ asked bluntly. "Surely our love has survived the passage of time. I thought I would never see you again and when I did, I felt my heart leaping in my chest." He paused and looked longingly at the woman by his side. "You said you thought you loved me, too."

"I did and I believed it for a moment or two, but..."

"But what, Emma?

"I don't belong here anymore," she said. "You have put down roots and you appear to be realising your ambitions and living the dream. I don't want to come back here to live permanently and a long-distance relationship wouldn't work, as we certainly haven't time to get to know each other again. Twenty years is a long time, BJ, or haven't you noticed?"

BJ sighed deeply. "You are breaking my heart all over again," he told her. "Daniel will be so disappointed that we won't be together as a family."

"I think he'll cope," she concluded.

"He had such high hopes, Emma. Doesn't it concern you that you are shattering his dreams?"

"And what are those dreams, BJ? He hasn't said anything to me about what he plans to do now that he's qualified. Has he discussed his plans with you?"

BJ shrugged. "Not really," he said nonchalantly. "I guess whatever he does, it will include Alison."

"For sure," Emma agreed. "And I don't think he'll return to Jamaica except for holidays, and to be honest, I haven't really given him the opportunity to discuss his plans with me. I've been too wrapped up in my own situation, selfish person that I am. He must have wondered why I haven't shown any interest in his future, or why I didn't suggest he fly home with me."

BJ smiled. "I don't think you're selfish, Emma. You eventually work out what's right to the benefit of everybody. Considering your own feelings isn't being selfish, as far as I can see. You have to do what is right for yourself, too." He paused deliberately and looked again into her eyes. "Are you sure you couldn't learn to love me again?"

Emma took his hand. "No, I'm not sure, BJ. I don't know how I feel. My heart fluttered like it used to when I saw you and then things happened to make me unsure again." She was thinking about Wayne and the thrill she had felt when he kissed her. *Telling BJ about Wayne isn't appropriate just now. Sitting so close to BJ reminds me how I used to feel about him and there is something deep inside that makes me see why I loved him. That is perhaps the wrong tense, and I should say love him. He is the father of my child, after all. Oh lord, I just don't know myself anymore.*

"Will you keep in touch with me at least?" he asked. "Now we are able to share Daniel, we ought to stay in communication. I will always love you, Emma, and as long as we are in touch, I will always have hope."

"I can't see any reason why we shouldn't keep in touch," she agreed. "But please don't cling to the hope that one day we'll be together again. I haven't got a crystal ball and I don't know how I'll feel tomorrow, or next week, or next year. Sitting here with you now shows me why we were good together, but I think I'm just stuck in a memory, and what happened in the past can't guarantee the future. There is a lovely lady waiting for you at home. Treat her kindly, BJ, and don't mess her around. If I know one thing about the female species, they don't respond kindly to being kept waiting, or feeling they are being used."

BJ shrugged and said nothing.

"I'll be in touch when I have got over the jet lag," she told him as he dropped her off at the Midland Hotel. "In spite of everything, BJ, it's been good to see you again." She winked mischievously. "Now I don't have to imagine how you have aged."

"Bitter sweet, Emma," he said pensively. "I won't give up hope, you know."

"But what about Gracie?"

"Gracie will be fine," he assured her. "She knows exactly where she stands with me."

Emma looked at him accusingly. "I don't think she does, BJ, and you aren't that considerate person anymore, the one I thought I knew. Do go back to being that person, please, for Gracie, and most of all, for yourself."

"If you were with me, that would be easy."

Emma sighed deeply. "Bye for now," she said as she got out of the car. "I'll be in touch."

BJ didn't reply and he drove away from the woman who still had a firm hold on his heart. He didn't look back. *Looking back will only prolong the agony,* he thought. *But I have to hope you'll be in my future, Emma.*

Fifteen

When BJ returned from dropping Emma off at the hotel, he found Gracie waiting for him. She was reclining on the settee and he gasped when he saw her. "Oh, Gracie," he whispered. "Don't do this to me just now."

"Do what?" she asked, smiling at the man she had allowed to take her heart, but her thoughts were clear in her head. *This guy could make me the happiest person in the world if he were to propose to me right here and now, but I must tread carefully. There is something going on with him and I'm as sure as I can be that it has something to do with the woman he has just dropped off in Birmingham.*

BJ's heart was beating fast. *Emma's rejection has left me fired up, and to see Gracie lying seductively on my sofa...* "Need you ask?"

Gracie needed no further encouragement. "I'm yours for the taking, BJ. I love you, but you already know that."

He walked over to her and took her in his arms. *I am doing something despicable and yet my carnal instincts are taking over.* "Oh, Gracie," he said hoarsely. "You have my head spinning and my heart beating so fast, and I want you so badly."

Gracie responded to his embrace and nuzzled his neck, kissing him enticingly until she found his waiting lips. "Take me, BJ," she whispered. "Take me with all the passion you have shown before. Take me and mean it..."

"Don't move," he instructed as he ripped off his own clothes and then sensually undressed her, slowly stroking her, kissing her, enjoying her groans and her writhing beneath him. He lifted her naked body and carried her to his bed as she continued to kiss his neck, his shoulder, his mouth, probing with her tongue until he cried out in ecstasy, releasing all the pent-up love for the woman he had seen walk out of his life less than an hour before.

Afterwards, he lay in silence next to the woman who had fulfilled his needs whenever he had desired, the woman who had never made any demands he wasn't able to meet, the gentle, loving woman he had used to his own ends. *What am I doing?* he asked himself silently as he listened to the gentle breathing of the beautiful lady by his side. *I don't deserve Gracie. She has been nothing but a sincere and loving friend to me, and here I am wishing she were somebody else. I hate myself, so how can I expect anybody to love me as I long to be loved? Gracie deserves more from me. Emma doesn't know if she could love me again and I am clinging to the hope Daniel will bring us together as a family. Am I asking too much?* He covered Gracie with the crisp white sheet on his bed and crept out of the room while she slept. Later, when he had formulated an interim plan, he woke her, invited her to take a shower and dress and he would take her out for dinner at Jambalaya. Afterwards, he took her to her own flat, kissed her on the cheek and said, "Goodnight, Gracie. I'll call."

~ * ~

The following morning, he woke to birds singing their autumn song in his garden. "Shut up," he shouted. "I'm not in a singing mood this morning." He made coffee and warmed croissants for breakfast. *I can't pretend I'm proud of myself,* he thought. *Today is the day Emma returns to Jamaica and I feel quite desolate in that she has rejected my love. It was so unwise to presume our love would stand the test of time. I felt sure being together as a family would make her see we could start again and have it all. How wrong could I have been?* Even in the shower, his thoughts went round and round in his head as he tried to make sense of his actions the previous day and night. *Emma knows about Gracie, but Gracie knows nothing about Emma—or does she? Gracie isn't stupid. I bet she deduced something was going on, since I wouldn't allow her to go with us when I drove Emma back to the hotel. And yet, she didn't say anything when I returned. She was there waiting for me.* He grabbed a towel and secured it round his waist. *How pathetic are you, BJ?* he asked himself as he went to his bedroom to dress. He sat on the side of the bed and stroked the sheet with a gentle hand. His thoughts surprised him. *Gracie was lying here yesterday and she made me feel so loved, when Emma didn't want a bar of it. Why am I so intent about denying Gracie my love when the woman who could have it all has shown little interest? I like Gracie...maybe I love her. Would it be wrong for me to marry her when there is a chance I might think I was dealing with second best?* He stood and returned his towel to the bathroom. Standing in all his naked glory, his thoughts were very clear. Throwing on some clothes, he went to the living room and picked up the phone. Looking at the instrument in his hand, he practised the words, "Gracie, will you marry me?"

Sixteen

Daniel met Emma at the hotel on Sunday morning after he had packed up his belongings and left them at the station, ready to pick up when he had seen his mother safely checked in at the airport. As they waited for their taxi, she suggested, "Shall we have lunch at the airport? It will mean we won't have to rush around afterwards."

"Sounds good to me," Daniel replied. "You seem happier today. I hope it's not because you are leaving."

Emma gave him a hug. "Not really, although it might be a relief to be away from all the stress and confusion I've experienced since I arrived here. You've put up with a lot from me since the degree ceremony. I'm sorry. I ought to have been more attentive to you. Oh, here's our cab."

Over lunch, the conversation was easy, and Emma felt more relaxed than she had felt for days. "I really have no idea what *your* plans are and now I'm going home..."

"Home?" Daniel repeated, asking a very pointed rhetorical question.

"I don't belong here anymore," she admitted.

"But what about Dad?"

"I couldn't give him a definitive answer," she said. "I've been very open with him, well, as open as I could be."

"Did you tell him about your Canadian guy?

"No."

"Why not? If you were open with him, I'd have thought Wayne would have been at the top of the agenda."

Emma sighed. "Our discussion led us away from that topic of conversation. Something happened and it interrupted us. Did you know BJ has a lady friend?"

Wide-eyed, Daniel had no need to answer to show Emma he didn't know, but he replied anyway. "That's a turn up for the books!" He grinned. "Pardon the pun. So where does that leave you?"

"You'll have to ask your father about that, but he insists he still loves me. Actually, I met the lady."

"You met her? Oh wow! That's a bit rich, isn't it? I mean, what did he say?" He tried to imitate BJ's voice. *'This is my past; here's my present.'*

Emma couldn't help but smile. "She didn't know who I was and she seemed very surprised at the colour of my skin. Just an observation, but I know the look. I've seen it so many times before."

Daniel laughed. "Oh lordy, lordy! Dad got himself a lady of colour! Cool, or what? Does that mean there is absolutely no chance of you and him getting together again? That's very sad, from my point of view."

Emma felt a little uncomfortable again. "I wish I could tell you either way, but I can't. Your dad and I are going to keep in touch. *You* are our joint concern now." She paused and looked directly at Daniel. "I'm assuming you aren't coming back to Jamaica?"

It was Daniel's turn to look sheepish. "Do you mind?" he asked.

"Of course I don't mind," she reassured him. "I'll miss you terribly, but I think I knew all along you would find work here."

Daniel shook his head slowly. "Why didn't I guess you would have it all sussed out?"

"Well, I'm not a psychic, so you'd better tell me more. I presume it involves Alison."

Daniel leaned back in his chair and breathed in deeply before he spoke. "First of all, I have secured a position with Liverpool City Council Social Services. It's a new post, so I'll have nobody to show me the ropes."

"That could be good, couldn't it?" Emma asked.

"Yes and no," he replied. "They've asked me to draw up a policy that will set out new procedures for assessing immigrants when they arrive in the UK. The post is experimental, but if it works, it may be adopted by other city councils and I might have to go to those places to train and mentor members of staff who are appointed to carry out the suggested methods of integration and the like. Legal immigrants should be straightforward. It's the illegal ones who might be more demanding. That part scares me a bit, but I think I have a few ideas about their situation. I'll just have to see where it takes me."

"Wow!" Emma exclaimed. "And you didn't think to tell me all this when I first arrived. What an absolute achievement for you! I am so proud of you, Dan."

"I wasn't offered the job until the day after degree day. When I returned to Halls, the letter was waiting for me. I opened it just before we left for The Lakes and as you know, things were a bit strained between us after that. I'm sorry. I know I should have told you sooner."

"Does your father know any of this?"

"No, he doesn't know about the job, but he does know I'm not going back to Jamaica. I asked him not to say anything to you. I wanted to tell you myself and…"

"... And you had worked out that I would be more than a little put out if you told him before you told me."

Daniel grinned. "You know me well, Mom, and you also know I would never deliberately upset you."

"Creep!" she said jokingly, as she poked him in the ribs. "I'll always be that soft touch, Dan! You are my boy and always will be. Now where does Alison fit in with all this? I know she has a teaching post in Liverpool so...? Is that why you applied for a job in the same city?"

"I applied first and Alison had so much confidence in me that she applied to Liverpool Education Authority for a teaching post. She has organised a flat for us to share..."

"Oh, my word! Things are moving fast. Just be careful, won't you? Look what happened to your father and me, and *we* weren't living together."

"Fear not, Mother dear. This is 1971 and society is more equipped to avoid unplanned pregnancies than you were in the fifties. These days there are ways and means of preventing babies being made too soon."

Emma laughed. "When did you become so grown up?"

"Since you taught me to stand on my own two feet and take everything in my stride. Thank you, Mom. I love you."

"I love you too, Dan," she said and then rapidly changing the subject, "I'll check in now and say my goodbyes. I don't like long farewells. Take care, my son. Let me have all the details of where you are living. Call me when you are settled."

Daniel watched as she disappeared through passport control, thankful his mother couldn't see the tear that had involuntarily trickled down his cheek.

~ * ~

Emma had parked her car at Kingston airport so she would have transport home without having to hail a cab. She had managed to catch forty winks during the flight and so she didn't feel as tired as she thought she might. When she arrived home, it was almost one o'clock in the morning and still hours from sunrise. *I haven't timed this very well,* she thought. *Maybe I should try to get some sleep, or I won't function very well during the day.* With that, she left her suitcase in the middle of the living room floor and went to bed.

She woke with a start. The phone was ringing, and for a moment, she wondered where she was. By the time she reached the phone, it had stopped. "Blimey! It's ten o'clock," she said out loud and thinking, *I must have been more tired than I thought. Whoever that was will have to call later.* She had breakfast and then showered. Feeling refreshed, she set about unpacking her case and put the washing machine on to make sure her clothes were washed and dried before she went back to work the following day.

A couple of hours later, when the telephone rang a second time, she answered it immediately. "Hi, Emma Williams."

"Where have you been? I called earlier just after ten and there was no reply."

"Hi, Ann! It's good to hear you, too!"

"Sorry, welcome home, Em. I was worried you hadn't arrived. I was sure you'd be up by ten and when you didn't answer the phone, I wondered if you'd decided to stay longer in England with Daniel."

Emma smiled to herself. "No, that wasn't an option, but I have so much to tell you and it's going to take a while, so give me an hour and then I'll come round and have a coffee with you. You won't believe what happened."

"Oh, my word! It sounds exciting. Give me a clue," Ann coaxed. "Daniel isn't back home with you, is he?"

"No clues and *exciting* isn't how I would describe it," Emma said. "And no, Daniel has a job in Liverpool, which I'll tell you about later. You'll just have to be patient."

"Aw, come on, Em. You know I was at the back of the queue when they handed out patience," Ann joked. "Can't you give me an itsy bitsy clue...*please,* Em."

Emma laughed. "Okay, but it has to be itsy bitsy, as you put it. Degree ceremony."

"What?" Ann scoffed. "Degree ceremony? That's why you went over there, isn't it? I already know that. Is that all you're giving me?"

"Take it or leave it, and if you don't get off the phone now, it will take longer for me to be ready to come to yours," Emma said. "See you in about an hour."

When she arrived at Ann's house, the coffee was ready and biscuits were on the table. "That was the longest hour I have ever watched tick by in my whole life," Ann grumbled. "You don't half know how to wind me up, Emma Williams."

"Who's rattled your cage this morning?" Emma teased. "Don't be getting annoyed with me as soon as I arrive home."

"I've missed you."

"I've only been away two weeks," Emma reminded her friend.

"And they've been the longest two weeks in my life...well, maybe not quite as long as those weeks we spent on the ship out here," Ann admitted. 'Come on, sit down and tell me all about it."

Seventeen

Having seen his mother safely checked in for her flight home, Daniel sat on the train in Birmingham New Street station and listened to the guard's whistle signalling the train's departure. His stomach lurched with excitement at the thought of seeing Alison again. *I have missed her more than I could ever have imagined.* He smiled to himself. *We must have been mad to have suppressed our true feelings for three years. What were we thinking? I knew how I felt about her and I thought she liked me. Wow! I love that girl.*

After almost two hours, the train pulled into Liverpool Lime Street station and as Daniel jumped down from the carriage, he spotted Alison straight away. She was running to meet him and she threw herself into his arms before he had time to retrieve his luggage. A friendly porter saw what was happening, took the two heavy suitcases from the carriage and placed them on the platform. "You'll be needing these, won't you, sir?"

Daniel grinned. "I will," he said. "Thank you, but you wouldn't put suitcases before a welcome like that, would you?"

The porter found a luggage trolley and loaded the cases onto it as Daniel felt in his pocket and found a half-crown, which he pushed into the porter's hand.

"Thank you very much, sir. Enjoy your stay."

Alison walked excitedly by Daniel's side as he pushed the trolley towards a waiting taxi. "I've missed you and you're going to love our flat. There must have been very clean and tidy students living there last year. It's spotless and we have everything we need."

"Sounds excellent," Daniel said smiling. *This girl is perfect,* he thought. *I am so lucky. We are going to have the perfect future together.*

~ * ~

Alison showed Daniel round their flat, almost dragging him from room to room in her enthusiasm. When she came to the first bedroom, she stopped at the door. "This is your room," she said seriously. "And the other is mine."

Daniel stared at her in astonishment. "Are we sleeping in separate rooms?"

Alison looked embarrassed. "Just for the first few weeks, or so."

"But why, Ali? We are a couple, aren't we? We are living together, aren't we? Why do we have to have separate rooms? It's not as though we haven't done it already, is it?"

"We are all of those things, but I've only just told Mum and Dad that we are seriously seeing each other," she told him. "They don't approve of sex before marriage and I don't want to advertise that we are sleeping together just yet."

"But they're not here, Ali. How will they know?"

Alison took his hand and led him to the living room to sit on the sofa. "My aunt in Southport, whose friend owns this flat, will be calling to see us any time without warning. She won't make an appointment...she'll just arrive unannounced. I don't want her to discover we are only using one bedroom, because she will certainly tell Mum and Dad if she thinks we are sleeping together."

Daniel was worried and it showed. "They do know I'm Black..."

"They know you are mixed race."

"And do they have a problem with that?"

"No, of course not!" she snapped. "Please don't make it an issue, Dan. I have always talked about you when I have been home during our time at uni. I told them all about you and that you were my best friend in Birmingham. More recently I told them you are BJ Johnson's son..."

"Oh lordy, lordy, Ali," he interjected. "Please tell me you explained I don't necessarily hold his views. Do they even know who he is?"

"They do and they have been to one of his lectures when he spoke in Edinburgh."

"Was that before or after they knew I'm his son?'

"It was about a year ago. Dad was more than interested because he has several West Indian nurses and doctors in his department and he wanted to make sure they were happy and settled in the hospital environment. He felt he might learn something from BJ as regards how his colleagues were feeling about living in a strange place." Alison took hold of Daniel's hand. "He didn't know at that point that you were his son, so he wasn't checking up on BJ, or on you. Dad has always been a good man-manager and he wanted to make sure he was doing what was required physically and psychologically for his staff. You have to believe me, Dan."

"I do believe you, Ali, but I wasn't anticipating any problems in our relationship. When you say you don't want to share my bed, I thought that was all part of being in love and living together."

"I know that, Dan? I love you with all my heart. You must know that without me telling you. There aren't any problems with us and there'll be none with my parents, but I just don't want them to know we are sleeping together, at least not until they are used to us being a couple," she told him earnestly. "I have to introduce you to them formally first."

"And when will that be?"

"As soon as they can arrange time off at the same time as each other. They were thinking about the end of September, early October when we have both settled into our jobs. Are you okay with that?"

"I'm fine," he told her. "Where will they stay?"

"They'll stay with my aunt and we'll arrange to see them either on a Saturday or Sunday or both."

Daniel, still holding her hand, pulled her close and nuzzled her hair. "Sorry I went into panic mode," he whispered. "Can we just prove our love for each other in our new home? I love you, Ali; I need you and I want you." He kissed her passionately, feeling her heart once again beating in time with his.

She sighed with longing and responded in the manner she hoped would show Daniel how serious she was in her love for him. "Who needs a bed?" she said, smiling, "when the sofa is big enough to..."

Urgently stripping off their clothes, they made love there and then, completely enveloped in their own bubble of romantic desire.

Eighteen

Emma and Ann sat at the kitchen table while Emma told her friend of the meeting with BJ at the degree ceremony.

"You mean he just turned up unannounced?" Ann asked.

"Unannounced to me," Emma confirmed. "But Daniel had been seeing him on a weekly basis for months."

Ann was shocked. "And he didn't tell you? The little devil! That's not like Daniel, is it?"

"Well, no, it isn't," Emma agreed. "But he's changed, Ann, and I can't decide if it's because he's just grown up and I hadn't noticed, or if BJ has changed Daniel's attitude in some way."

"Do you really think BJ would do that?"

"Not deliberately," Emma admitted. "He might have suggested we should get together as a family, though. Dan was so eager for us to be 'normal,' as he put it."

"What?" Ann gasped. "What about your family here? And what about Wayne?"

Emma sighed. "Well, that's another thing for me to ponder. I have to decide if I still love BJ enough to uproot myself from all that I adore here, or whether my new-found attachment to Wayne is what I want and need. I'm so confused, Ann."

"Blood and sand, Em!" Ann wailed. "I hadn't realised you still had strong feelings for BJ. I thought you were over him, especially when Wayne came into the picture. What a dilemma, but I know what I would do."

"Tell me then, because I don't know if I'm on my head or my heels at the moment."

"I know it's easy for me to say, because I haven't met BJ, but I can see Wayne thinks the world of you. He called me three times while you were away, just to talk to me because I'm your friend. He's got it bad, Em."

"Oh, please don't say that, Ann. I like him a lot, more than a lot, but how can I be sure he's not on the rebound? It will take more than a few weekends to make us know if we're right together. I'm not prepared to fall madly in love with him yet. I can't have my heart broken again, and adding the situation with BJ into the mix makes it much more complicated for me."

"Why?"

Emma looked squarely at her friend. "Because I kept feeling those elusive butterflies when I was close to him and yet they didn't last long and I couldn't see me going back to live over there just because of butterflies in my belly! To counteract all that, there's another woman involved with BJ and I saw that she's in love with him, but he insisted to me that he isn't in love with her. And, to tell you the important bit—she's Black."

"Emma Williams! Colour has never been an issue for you," Ann retorted. "So why do you have to bring that into the equation?"

"Because I'm convinced BJ still has a problem with being seen in public with a white woman."

"You are joking, of course," Ann scoffed.

"No, I'm not," Emma explained. "He was fine when we went out to lunch with Daniel and his girlfriend—"

"Girlfriend?"

"Don't interrupt. I'll get to that later. When Daniel and Alison went off to celebrate with their friends after the degree ceremony, BJ was struggling to find a place where we might talk away from prying eyes."

"Did he say that?" Ann asked.

"Well, not in so many words, but he asked me back to his house and I panicked in case he wanted to get me there to…"

"Aw, come on, Em," Ann said bluntly. "From what you told me, that's what you and he were hungry for in the old days!"

Emma dared to smile. "Yes, we were," she admitted quietly. "But while my heart fluttered like it used to when I first saw him, I had to wrestle with all the hurt he caused and I realised we have both changed. We've grown older, and with that comes maturity and common sense, if I might be so bold as to suggest that. We live in different worlds now. He has become very Anglicised, and I'm more Jamaican than I realised. I didn't fit in, Ann. I felt like an intruder in an alien world. I was totally out of my depth in the English way of life. BJ, Daniel and Alison, who is Scottish by the way, were so in tune with the British lives they are leading and I seem to have lost my Englishness."

"All this sounds too complicated to me," Ann said. "Either you love him or you don't."

Emma grimaced at the thought. "Here's the thing," she said. "I love BJ because he's the father of my son. I saw all the qualities I fell in love with in the first place, but I didn't experience that comfortable feeling I have when I'm with Wayne."

"So why can't you decide who you'd rather be with?" Ann asked. "It seems pretty obvious to me."

Emma reached across the table to hold Ann's hand. "When you say it like that, it's obvious to me, too, but you don't have to make the choice, my friend. I have such a lot of baggage to contend with. Looking at it in black and white—pardon the terminology—it seems Wayne is the obvious choice. And to make an outrageous analogy, he's white and BJ is..."

"Don't go down that route, Em," Ann warned as she removed her hand from Emma's grip. "You've never had an issue with colour. Why start now?"

"Because it has made itself an issue since I met Wayne," she admitted. "I think I feel comfortable with him because I don't have to worry about..." She stopped abruptly. "Oh Ann, I'm sorry," she wailed. "I'm being insensitive and disrespectful to you and Earl. I didn't think. Please forgive me."

Ann regarded her friend with questioning eyes. "What on earth are you talking about?" she asked. "Do you think you're offending me because I'm in a mixed race relationship? You know I'm happy with my lot. I never had a problem with Earl, and my kids have grown up to be comfortable in their skin. I know they feel very special having a white mother and a Black father. Why bring us into your problems?"

Emma shifted in her seat. "I'm not bringing you into my problems, Ann. Please don't think that," she said. "It's just that the analysis of my situation made it look like I was saying it's easier having a partner of the same colour and I really don't think that at all. I never did and I never would." She looked at Ann in an effort to read her mind. "I've upset you, haven't I?"

Ann sighed. "Look, Em. I can see now why you're so confused and I certainly don't want to add to your problems. It's clear to me you need time on your own to decide which way you want to go. *I* can't tell you. It's something you'll have to decide for yourself."

Emma was completely overcome with sadness and it showed. "Oh Ann," she cried. "My trip to the home country has turned out to be my nemesis. I went back there with such enthusiasm in seeing where Daniel had been for the past three years and I came back with the worries of the world on my shoulders. Now, it looks like I've tarnished our relationship, yours and mine, because of the unreasonable demands I've placed on myself."

"Perhaps you should go home now and look at the pros and cons for both Wayne and BJ," Ann suggested pointedly. "It's a terrible way to decide who's going to be your life partner, but you need some sort of basis upon which to form your answer. I don't envy you one little bit. If I can give you one piece of advice, though, don't let your heart rule your head this time. A few moments ago, you said something about becoming more sensible as you've grown older. In my opinion, you aren't being sensible at all. You're allowing your heart to rule your head big time and you have to start looking at your *own* needs, not Daniel's, not Wayne's and not BJ's. What is it you need to make you happy and contented for the rest of your life? You have to decide that yourself. Nobody else can do it for you."

Emma sat in silence and listened to what Ann was saying. She waited a moment before she spoke. "Are you deserting me in my hour of need?" she asked.

Ann gasped and stood with her hands on her hips, unusually unleashing a tirade of harsh words in Emma's direction. "I've had it with you at the moment, Emma. I have always been here for you. I've backed you in all of your schemes, even if I thought they were harebrained, helped you when you had nobody else to turn to and I have always been your best friend in the whole world, but you aren't the person I knew and loved before you went on this jolly to the home country. You would never have brought racial differences into any of our conversations other than to emphasise our acceptance of equality. How could you have the gall to suggest I'm deserting you? If you ask me, BJ has got into your head and manipulated you to his own ends. How Daniel fits in with all this,

I have no idea, but I suggest you go away and think very seriously about it."

Emma looked wide-eyed at the woman whom she had thought was her friend for life. "I don't know what to say, Ann," she said quietly. "I think I'd better leave." She rose from her chair and walked towards the door. "See yer," she said with very little certainty or conviction at all and left, leaving a very sad friend in her wake.

Nineteen

After her contretemps with Ann, Emma returned to her own house in tears. *I have never had a difference of opinion with Ann. Why does she choose now to tell me how she really feels?* She splashed cold water on her face and looked at herself in the mirror. *Oh my! Just look at me. Misery, turmoil and dejection personified. Only you can put this right, my girl. Give Ann and yourself time to calm down and then...* She was interrupted by her phone ringing. *Oh damn! Not now...*"Emma Williams."

"Welcome home, Em. I have missed you so much..."

"Wayne!" she crooned with forced animation. "So good to hear you. How are you?"

"What's wrong?" Wayne asked. "I can tell something's not right."

"Nothing wrong," she said, trying to raise her mood to what might pass for *happy-to-hear-you.* "Good to hear your voice..." Then the tears came again.

Wayne's voice was low. "Emma, tell me what's wrong. Is it me? Have I done something to upset you? Should I have called you earlier? Are you sad to be home? What is it?"

Emma breathed in deeply in an effort to control her emotions. "No, it's not you," she sobbed. "It's me! I have upset Ann and I don't know how to put it right."

"Oh dear," Wayne sympathised. "Friends bicker all the time. I'm sure it will sort itself out soon. How did your trip go?"

That question set Emma off again. "Don't ask me that at the moment," she wailed. "It was telling Ann about the trip that caused the disagreement..."

"That bad, hey?"

"No, not bad in the real sense of the word, more confusing for me than anything else."

"Do you want to talk about it?' Wayne asked. "I'm a good listener and I won't judge, I promise."

"Have you got a few days to stay on the phone?" she asked, trying to inject a little humour in the conversation.

"Not really, but things have been happening here while you've been away. My divorce is finalised and I'm a free man."

"Congratulations. I'm happy for you, even though I might not sound it at the moment."

"I have so much to tell you, but the most important thing is that I'm selling up and coming to live in Jamaica."

Emma gasped. "Oh," she said.

There was silence at the other end of the line and then, "Say something, Em. I thought you'd be pleased."

"That sounds good..."

"Is that all you have to say? I was hoping you'd be pleased I would be there permanently. You did agree we had something going between us, didn't you? We discussed it on numerous occasions, even though I know you aren't ready to fully commit just now. Now I'm not so sure," Wayne said, his voice lacking the enthusiasm he had displayed when Emma first answered her phone.

"Where are you planning to live?" Emma asked bluntly.

"I haven't planned so far ahead yet," he admitted, "but I'm sure we can sort something out between us, can't we?"

Emma was becoming distraught again. "I can't discuss this at the moment, Wayne. I have too much going on in my head and it's not something I want to talk about over the phone."

"Are you giving me the brush-off, Emma?" he asked. "If you are, tell me now before I make a bigger fool of myself than I have already."

Emma grabbed her forehead with her free hand. "What are you talking about?" she blurted. "I'm not giving you the brush-off, as you put it. I just can't talk about my problems over the phone. I need to see you, but I'm not ready for you to move permanently into my life just yet. I thought you understood that. It's too much too soon for me...for us, Wayne, but I still want to see where our relationship leads us. Your coming here to live will put pressure on us both. Is that what you were planning to do?"

"Of course not!" he said. "What has happened to you, Em? Something obviously went on in England..." He stopped abruptly as he realised what it might be. "BJ?" he questioned.

Emma didn't answer.

"Oh, it seems I've hit the nail on the head, doesn't it?" he said resignedly. "I can't compete with BJ Johnson, Emma, especially since he's the father of your son. What do you want me to do? I can't be...no, I *won't* be second best again." He paused. "I can't make up your mind for you, Em. That's something you'll have to do for yourself."

Emma was in tears again. "That's what Ann said, too," she sobbed. "I am so confused and I didn't want to talk about this over the phone. It looks like I have lost you both and I don't know what to do about it."

Wayne sighed loudly and deeply. "I guess you need time," he told her quietly. "I can't say I'm happy about it, but I'll come to Jamaica in a couple of weeks and hope by then you have some clarity in your situation. I'll stay with Chas and Mimi. I'm sure they won't mind and you needn't worry about my moving too fast in our relationship. You certainly put me straight about that the first time we kissed. I heard you loud and clear then, Em, and I understand where you were coming from now, but I also know how we both felt in that intimate moment and I'd like to pursue those feelings if and when you're ready."

"I don't deserve you," Emma told him quietly.

"The Emma I have got to know deserves love in her life," he said matter-of-factly. "The Emma I'm listening to at the moment needs to find her way through the grey clouds into the sunshine again. I'll see you in a couple of weeks, no strings attached."

"Thanks, Wayne, she said. "Like I said, I don't deserve you."

Twenty

Daniel's meeting with Alison's parents didn't happen until early December. Nor had the expected unannounced visit from Alison's aunt materialised. With Liverpool city centre lit up for Christmas and a dusting of powdery snow adorning the pavements, Alison and Daniel prepared to meet Mr and Mrs Macdonald in the Adelphi Hotel for lunch on the first Saturday in December.

"How do I look?" Daniel asked Alison before they left the flat. "Do you think I should wear a suit, or will casual be okay?"

"Smart casual is fine," Alison told him. "You aren't going to meet the king and queen."

"I know, but I want to give a good impression, Ali," he said. "I'm nervous. I don't mind admitting it."

Alison went to give him a hug. "Don't be nervous, Dan. They're not going to eat you, nor bombard you with questions."

"How can you be sure about that? They'll want to know who has fallen in love with their daughter and they'll also want to make sure I'm worthy of you."

Alison shook her head in dismay. "Don't be silly," she said smiling. "They'll love you almost as much as I do."

Daniel decided on dark grey slacks, pale blue shirt and navy blue fine-knit sweater. He put a tie in Alison's handbag. "Just in case I feel under-dressed when we're in the Adelphi Hotel."

When they arrived at the hotel, both wrapped in winter coats and college scarves advertising their adored Birmingham university colours, the Macdonalds were waiting at the top of the steps. Alison let go of his hand and ran to greet them. "Hi," she said happily. "Welcome to Liverpool. Have you been waiting long?"

Her parents hugged her warmly. "Not long," her mother told her as she looked over her daughter's shoulder at the young man who had followed closely behind as Alison ran up the steps. "And this is Daniel, I presume."

"The one and only," Alison said as she introduced the man in her life to her parents. "Mum, Dad, this is Daniel Williams. Dan, my mum and dad."

Daniel shook hands with them both. "I'm pleased to meet you, Mr and Mrs Macdonald. I have heard so much about you."

"And we are happy to meet you, too, aren't we, Stuart?" Mrs Macdonald replied cheerily. "And please, Mr and Mrs is so formal. I'm Isla and this is Stuart."

Stuart grinned. "I'll answer to anything," he joked. "And you are so like your father. I met him, you know."

Daniel looked wide-eyed at Stuart. "I had no idea!" he said. "Alison told me you'd been to one of his lectures, but she didn't say you'd actually met him."

"That's because I didn't know," Alison admitted. "You didn't tell me you had actually spoken to BJ, Dad."

"Oh, BJ is it? There was a reception after the lecture and I was invited by the organisers to attend. It was only a brief meeting and it's unlikely he'll remember me," Stuart explained. "Anyway, when did you become on such familiar terms with the esteemed writer?"

"Since we went out for lunch on degree day," Alison explained. "It was all very informal, as I hope this lunch is going to be. No coming over as the protective father and all that. You might scare Dan away."

Isla jumped in amiably. "No, he won't. I like Daniel already, so he's made one friend in the family."

They all laughed. "There you are, Dan," Alison reassured him. "On that note, let's go and eat. I'm starving."

Over lunch, the conversation was light and easy. Amicable discussions about what they were eating inevitably turned to comparisons of English/Scottish/ Jamaican cuisines and Daniel joined in happily. "I'm lucky to have sampled all three," he said. "My English mother serves both Jamaican and English dishes. She likes to hang on to her British roots as she's living in Jamaica, and Alison has tried to introduced me to *neeps* and *tatties* and *Cullen skink*, not to mention the *haggis* she keeps on urging me to try."

"And have you tried it?" Stuart asked.

"Not yet," he said smiling. "I keep on thinking it might be like English black pudding and the mere thought of eating the fat and blood of any animal turns my stomach. I am convinced *haggis* might be like that."

Stuart laughed. "How do you think I feel when I'm removing body parts from humans at work and then going home to eat chopped liver, heart and oatmeal all stuffed into a sheep's stomach?"

"Not funny, Dad," Alison interjected, "I'll never get Dan to try haggis now. Thank you very much."

"I might just be brave enough sometime in the not-too-distant future," Daniel told them. "If I'm going to be part of a Scottish family…" *Oh, my lord,* he thought. *What am I saying?*

Alison came to the rescue. "Plenty of time before we start thinking in those terms," she said, laughing to make light of what Daniel had suggested. "Come on, Dan. We'll go and settle the bill."

"You will do no such thing," Isla snapped. "This is our treat. You two have only just started bringing home the bacon."

"That's a saying I haven't heard for a while,' Alison said. "Have you ever heard that before, Dan?"

Daniel grimaced and shrugged, and surprised himself when the thought popped into his head. *Oh heck. Didn't Mom say Dad shrugged when he wasn't quite sure how to answer? Better answer quickly.* "To be honest, I haven't heard it used in conversation, but I seem to remember my high school English teacher introducing us to English idiom. The phrase isn't new to me and I know my mom hasn't used it when talking to me, so I'll have to thank Mr Merrick for providing me with that snippet of information."

With the bill settled, they retrieved their coats and as they left the restaurant, Isla asked Alison if they might look at the department stores. "I'd love to go in Lewis's and George Henry Lee's. Do you mind, Stuart? I know you don't like wandering around the shops."

"I don't mind at all, but what about Daniel? He might like shopping—"

"No, I don't," Daniel interrupted. "Maybe you and I can walk down to the Pier Head. It's really interesting down there."

"I'll tell you where I *would* like to go," Stuart told him eagerly. "I would really like to see the two cathedrals—the prestigious Anglican Cathedral and the Metropolitan Cathedral of Christ the King—commonly known as Paddy's Wigwam, I believe. Both built in vastly different architectural styles. Do you know how to get to them, Dan? You don't mind if I call you Dan, do you?"

"Not at all," Daniel replied. "I'd be delighted if you did. And in answer to your first question, I know the cathedrals are situated at either end of Hope Street. Rather appropriate, don't you think?"

Stuart nodded. "It is indeed." He turned to his wife and said, "We'll see you two back here in a couple of hours. Does that give you enough time to spend all my money?"

~ * ~

As they walked to Hope Street from the hotel, Stuart asked Daniel if he had been apprehensive about meeting Alison's parents..."especially me, her protective father?" he added with a grin.

"I'd be lying if I said I wasn't, but not now," Daniel told him amicably.

"Why not now?" Stuart continued.

"Because I have found you to be friendly and accepting."

"And is that how you judge people?" Stuart asked.

Daniel was taken aback. "I hope I'm not giving you the impression I'm judgmental," Daniel said warily. "My mom would be appalled if she thought I might make rash assessments of the people I meet."

"But don't you have to make a quick assessment of the people you meet for the first time...like your dad says in his lectures? He seemed to be very much aware of his ethnicity."

Daniel felt his face becoming hot, even though the air was freezing cold. "BJ's views aren't necessarily mine, Mr Macdonald. His views were a problem when he met my mom, but she has always instilled in me that a person cannot and must not be judged by the colour of their skin." He paused self-consciously. "I presume that's what we are discussing here."

Stuart looked a little uncomfortable and Daniel noticed. "Look, I'm sorry, Dan. The fact that you just called me Mr

Macdonald suggests I have made you feel as uncomfortable as I am feeling at the moment. I truly have no problem with the colour of anybody's skin, particularly yours. If I've given the impression I have such problems, I apologise profusely."

"No need to apologise," Daniel told him. "I am and have always been proud of my mixed heritage. If Alison were here, she would be upholding my position as a member of this multicultural society we live in. She often fought my corner at uni when people tried to highlight my differences." He smiled. "I hope her views reflect those of you and Isla."

"They certainly do, and again, I'm sorry if I made you feel ill at ease."

"You didn't," Daniel assured him. "Alison said you wouldn't be concerned about the colour of my skin and she also told me that you attended my dad's lecture in order to better understand your Black colleagues. I appreciate that."

Stuart coughed to hide his embarrassment and then asked, "Are you and Alison in a serious relationship? I have to ask. I know she has liked you for years!" He laughed. "After her first term in Birmingham, she came home for Christmas and never stopped talking about you—*this interesting boy from Jamaica who was not only good looking, but kind and sociable and unassuming in every way.* You mentioned being accepted a few moments ago and just to put you straight, you are."

Daniel had to smile. "Wow! I have something to live up to then," he said. "And yes, we are serious about each other. Do I have your permission to continue with our courtship?"

Stuart laughed. "That's very formal, *Mr Williams.*" He winked. "I approve and so does Isla. I could tell as soon as you said hello to her. Now we can relax and study the architecture of GG Scott, Lutyens, and Gibberd."

"Goodness, you are very well informed," Daniel said in admiration of Stuart's knowledge. "The only thing I've learned about the Anglican cathedral is that it isn't yet complete. It was started in 1902 and there is still work to be done before it will be complete and ready for the official opening. The Catholic cathedral was completely planned and built between 1962 and 1967. I really don't know what we should glean from that."

"That Catholics know what they want and go out and get it?" Stuart suggested facetiously. "Do you go to church, Dan?"

"I'm afraid I don't," Daniel admitted. "My mom decided she couldn't reconcile all the horrors of war, nor the wrong-doings of society with an all-loving God. She claims to be a Humanist, but she bases her morals and life in general on Christian ethics. I tend to feel the same, although she never pushed me in any particular religious direction. What about you, Stuart?"

Stuart dug his hands in his pockets and declared solemnly, "I'm a lapsed Catholic, and after what you have just said, I might just call myself a Humanist, too. I value people's well-being and dignity. My job is to care for and tend to the sick in order to give them a better quality of life." He gave Daniel an affectionate pat on the back. "Here we are—Anglicans first!"

~ * ~

Later that evening, when Alison and Daniel were back in their flat, they snuggled on the settee and watched *Sunday Night at the London Palladium*. Jimmy Tarbuck, a Liverpudlian, had taken over from Bruce Forsyth as compere and Alison commented, "It's a good thing we're getting used to the Liverpool accent, isn't it? Otherwise we'd have trouble understanding Jimmy Tarbuck." She wriggled as she made herself comfortable. "By the way, did Dad give you the grilling you expected?" Alison asked casually.

"He did!" Daniel said emphatically. "I doubt he'll want to see me again after the answers I gave him."

Alison sat bolt upright. "What? Did he offend you?"

Daniel looked seriously at his girlfriend and blew out his breath indignantly. "Well, he said I would need a lot of courage to take you on and I had to make sure you didn't try to blackmail me with doe eyes and whimpering, so I told him where to get off, talking about my girlfriend like that." He grinned and winked.

"Daniel!" Alison exclaimed. "He said nothing of the sort! You devil! I could tell he liked you when we saw you waiting for Mum and me back at the Adelphi. Your body language was that of best buddies."

Daniel laughed. "Are you going to say *I told you so?* He was very accepting and he gave me his blessing to carry on seeing you!"

"Okay, *I told you so*, but that's just as well," Alison told him happily. "We're living together, aren't we?"

"We certainly are!" Daniel beamed as he took her in his arms, nuzzled her hair and whispered in her ear, "I love you, Ali, with all my heart and soul."

Twenty-one

Two weeks after her run-in with Ann, Emma determined she should be the one to try to patch things up with her best friend. When she telephoned the Brown household on Saturday afternoon, Glory answered. "Oh hi, Auntie Em. Do you want Mom?"

"I do," Emma answered.

A few moments passed before Glory replied. "Auntie Em, I'm going to be honest with you. Mom is frantically shaking her head, saying she doesn't want to talk, but she's done nothing but bewail the state of your friendship for the past two weeks and I'm telling the pair of you now, *SORT IT OUT!* I'm giving the phone to Mom now. See you later, Auntie Em."

Emma waited with bated breath. She heard Ann breathing heavily and instantly decided she must be the one to break the ice. "I'm sorry," she said. "I am truly, truly sorry. I had no right to unload all my problems on you, and I went about it in totally the wrong way. Please don't be mad at me any longer, Ann. I can't bear not being able to talk to you, see you, and go back to normal..."

"Oh, shut up and stop gabbling, Em," Ann said. "Let's start over and why don't you come round for a cuppa? I've missed you, and you didn't really tell me about your trip other than you saw BJ. You never told me about Daniel and his girlfriend either, so I'm waiting. See you in ten minutes."

Emma breathed a sigh of relief. "I'll be round in five," she said happily.

"Don't you drive too fast, Em. I want you to arrive in one piece, not in little pieces in a box!"

"God, Ann, don't be so morbid, but I'm glad we can snipe at each other again without taking offence. See you in ten then!"

~ * ~

"It's wonderful how a cup of tea will cure all ills," Ann said as they once again sat at the kitchen table to put the world to rights. "Let's not fall out again, Em. It isn't good for my constitution, and Earl would have killed me if I'd gone on much longer chewing off his ear!"

"I'm so sorry," Emma apologised again.

"And stop apologising," Ann demanded. "I know you're sorry and I forgive you, but having said that, I'm sorry too for not being more understanding. Normally, I would have listened and tried to help, but you did choose the wrong time of the month for me and PMT was in full flow, if you'll pardon the expression."

"Oh my, how I have missed our chats, the frivolous ones and the serious," Emma told her.

Ann nodded. "Now," she said seriously. "Tell me about BJ and Wayne and who's in the lead in the race to your heart."

"Oh, stop it, Ann," Emma protested mildly. "I have really tried not to get myself tied up in knots about it. It is what it is. My dealing with it has isolated me from everybody. You and I have never fallen out like that and BJ was as confused as I was, I think. It was obvious he was sleeping with his girlfriend, although he didn't admit it. That in itself made me see a different person from the BJ I left behind. He kept saying he loved me and not Gracie." She paused and inhaled deeply. "How could he treat her like that?"

Ann smiled in an effort to show Emma she was on her side, but her words seemed to contradict her facial expression. "You know, Em," she offered. "I understand what you're saying, but you have really..." She paused deliberately. "I'm trying to find the right word so as not to trivialize what I want to say. Maybe, just maybe, you have glorified sex in your own mind. I'm not saying making love is to be dismissed as something and nothing, because when you truly love the person you're with, sex is loving and sensual and satisfying. It cements your feelings for that person and I want you to know I understand that."

"I remember we had a similar conversation when we were coming out here," Emma reminded her.

"I know, and that's what I'm trying to say again," Ann explained gently. "Men sometimes view sex differently. Their libido is the driving force, if you'll pardon the expression again. I tried to explain to you about the guys during the war. They used me for their own pleasure before they went to the Front and I let them. Earl knows that. We don't have secrets, but I knew Earl was different; I just knew. He had sex with other girls before me, but he knew, too, that *I* was different. That's love for yer!"

"But I can't believe that BJ is driven by his libido. Surely he must love Gracie to make love to her, I presume on a regular basis."

"How do you know he does?" Ann asked.

Emma shrugged. "I don't," she admitted. "When she went to his house while I was there, she seemed so comfortable in his home, when I wasn't. She talked to him like he meant a lot to her. It was just a feeling I got. Surely gut feelings are more often right than wrong."

"It's a hard one, Em," Ann told her. "I don't know these people, so I can't agree nor disagree."

"I asked him straight out if he had slept with her…"

"You didn't!"

"I did!"

"And what did he say?"

Emma sighed. "He said I didn't need to know, but I felt I did in order to work out whether he loved her or not. As it turned out, it didn't help at all, since I was just basing my answer on gut feelings."

Ann stood and went to give Emma a hug. "Has all this talking helped you sort out your feelings, Em? I hope it's helped a bit."

"Well," Emma said pensively. "I don't think it's BJ I need to be with now, but when I spoke to Wayne, it was just after you and I…well, you know…" She inhaled deeply. "Well, I was a mess and I seem to have alienated him, too."

"Bloody hell, Emma," Ann blurted. "How did you do that? That guy would move heaven and earth for you, even I know that."

"I was in such a state and he sort of detected I had seen BJ. I couldn't give him a straight answer and I was blubbering all through the call. He did tell me his divorce came through and he's planning on coming here to live."

Ann nodded. "I know that. He told me when he called while you were away. I didn't know about the divorce, though."

"We haven't spoken since. I'm just hoping he'll let me know when he arrives. It must be any day now."

"He will," Ann told her. "Even I can be sure about that, so you have your act up to scratch, Em. The ball will be in your court, and no more confusion, for gawd sake! And you still haven't told me about Daniel's girlfriend, but that will keep until next time. I'll have to get Earl's dinner on now. Will you stay and eat with us?"

"No thanks, Ann. Maybe next time. I must get home in case Wayne calls. See yer later."

Twenty-two

Before BJ called Gracie, he had held the phone to his ear and practised his proposal. "Gracie, will you marry me?" He listened to himself and grimaced. *I can't act on impulse. I'm not an impulsive guy. I'll wait until Emma contacts me as she promised. Maybe leaving Daniel and me here in England might show her how much she is missing.*

~ * ~

In Jamaica, Emma was waiting for Wayne to call. Every time her phone rang, her heart beat faster and she had been disappointed when it wasn't Wayne on the other end of the line. The couple of weeks Wayne had allowed to elapse before his trip to Jamaica had dragged, and Emma was resigning herself to the fact that he might have got cold feet and decided she was too high maintenance for him to be in a long term relationship. *Perhaps he's decided I'm not worth getting to know,* she thought sadly. *Maybe I should try calling Chas to see if Wayne's plans are still the same. Would it be too forward of me to call Wayne myself? Are we close enough for me to do that?* She tried to answer the questions for herself. *I'm sure he wouldn't mind if I called him. Maybe that's what he's waiting for. I didn't exactly give him any encouragement when he called me. I more or less told him I was choosing between BJ and him. Well done, me!* She sat in her garden and inspected the pristine lawn and straight lines she had made and smiled to herself. *Who else would insist upon those lines in the garden? Only me. One of my foibles.* The mention of foibles triggered thoughts of BJ. *Has BJ any foibles? Do I know anything about him—I mean really know about him? What's his favourite food? I have no idea and yet I know that Wayne loves Jamaican rum cake. BJ shrugs a lot, but Wayne always has an answer ready to explain this and that. Would it be sensible to pursue a relationship with Wayne when I have only seen him on and off, albeit for almost a year now? On the other hand, would it be sensible to go back to BJ just because he is the father of my son? Is that enough to sustain a full time relationship? Is my respect for him still the same as before? I don't think it is. I saw a side of him that was alien to me. He's selfish...* She paused in her thoughts and said out loud, "Selfish? Well, so am I, I guess. Aren't we all selfish to a certain extent?" She sighed, a long, deep sigh which seemed to come from the bottom of her soul.

~ * ~

In Stratford-Upon-Avon, BJ Johnson immersed himself in his writing. He didn't contact Gracie or Emma. Daniel called him regularly and they maintained a healthy relationship. "How's the job going?" he asked.

"Good!" Daniel enthused. "I haven't submitted my plans to the head of department yet, but she monitors my progress and is happy so far. Once my scheme is finalised, we'll submit it to the Home Office for approval. Once we are given the go-ahead, we'll gradually put my ideas into practice. Only then will we be able to see if it works."

"I'm very proud of you," BJ told him. "I never thought I would have the opportunity to tell my son that."

"Thanks, Dad," Daniel said. "I didn't think I would ever hear those words from my dad, either. I'm so pleased we made contact. Have you heard from Mom?"

"No, I haven't, but I guess she is settling back into her Jamaican life. I don't want to pressure her, so I'm leaving it up to her to call me."

"That's very noble of you," Daniel offered. "And also sensible, I might say. What's happening in your world now that the excitement of degree day and seeing Mom again is over?"

BJ wondered how much he should tell Daniel. "Well, my life does not stand still, that's for sure. I have friends whom I see fairly regularly..."

Daniel grasped his opportunity. "Does that include your lady friend?" he asked without ceremony.

"Oh, my lord!" BJ exclaimed. "I should have known Emma would say something about Gracie to you. Is it a problem for you?"

"No, of course not," Daniel quickly replied. "I would have thought it might be a problem for you, though."

"Well, it is and it isn't."

"How do you mean?"

BJ thought for a moment before he spoke. "I'm not sure I should explain it to you, Dan—no offence meant. I really don't want Emma to have information that might affect how she regards me. She has met Gracie and has already surmised things that I have neither confirmed nor denied. I'm still hoping Emma will change her mind, but to be honest, I have been seriously thinking I'm being too optimistic."

"Mom already knows about Gracie, so why should it affect how she thinks?" Daniel reasoned. "If *you* think about it, Dad, keeping secrets about your affair with Gracie is reminiscent of the affair you had with Mom. I'm not being judgmental, but..."

"...but in a way you are," BJ told him. "I—we—are in a very complicated situation which I'm sure you totally understand. I keep thinking if your mom finds she misses you and me while she is in Jamaica, then I might still hope she is thinking about us—me, you and herself—being a family, just like you dream about."

Daniel didn't reply.

"Are you still there, son?"

"I am," Daniel answered. "I'm not sure I agree with your reasoning, though. For one thing, I'm living with Alison now and that isn't going to change whether Mom is here or not, so the family unit won't be as I envisioned as a child. Secondly, how can you say you love Mom and then carry on seeing Gracie? Mom told me that as well, so please don't be shocked."

"I thought she might keep that to herself," BJ said. "And I feel very uncomfortable talking about Gracie to you. I think it's too personal a topic, and much as I love you, son, I don't think I should involve you in what is happening in my love life. Can we steer this conversation in another direction?" He paused before he added, "It sounds as though you are very serious about Alison."

"I am," Daniel said. "We're saving to buy a house together."

"Wow! That is serious. Let me know when you are ready to move in and I'll give you a hand."

Daniel laughed. "It will be a while yet. The student accommodation we're renting at the moment will be fine for the next year or so, but thanks. I'll remember your offer."

BJ wound up the conversation. "I must go, Dan. Places to go, people to see. Thanks for calling. We'll speak again next week."

"Sure will," Daniel agreed. "See you, Dad. Bye."

~ * ~

It was Wednesday soon after she arrived home from work when Wayne called. "Hi," he said quietly. "Is it safe for me to call?"

Emma smiled to herself. "Of course. How are you?"

"More to the point, how are you?" Wayne asked. "I know I caught you at a bad time previously. Did you sort out your problems with Ann?"

"I did and I need to apologise to you, too. I had no right to unload my problems on you and I know I gave you the impression that I don't want to see you..."

"I didn't say anything about that, Emma."

"No, but *I* did," she admitted. "I let you believe it was a contest between you and BJ as to whom I wanted to be with and I can truly tell you there is no contest. I came back to Jamaica totally confused because BJ appeared like a bolt out of the blue and..." She stopped suddenly. "Are you here in Kingston?" she asked.

"I am."

"Then please, will you come round for dinner? I would much prefer to talk to you face to face." She heard a gasp from the guy at the other end of the line. "Wayne?"

"Yes," he answered. "And yes, I'll come round. I'm just so surprised you want to see me again. I had almost given up hope after our last conversation."

"See you at six then," she said. "Bye!" Smiling to herself, she put down the phone and went into the kitchen, dancing to the tune of "Chatanooga Choo Choo" playing in her head.

Twenty-three

BJ thought long and hard about what Daniel had said to him regarding Gracie. *My son questioned my feelings for both his mother and for Gracie.* He also recalled that Emma had said he had changed and he wasn't considerate anymore. *Emma talked about being selfish, too, and I have to admit, I am being and have been selfish. I have convinced myself that being honest with Gracie about my feelings gives me the right to accept her love without loving in return.* He made himself a cup of coffee and went to sit on the sofa, the sofa where he had succumbed to Gracie's sensuousness a couple of weeks before. *Gracie loves me and she has never let me down. Emma, on the other hand, walked out on me, and not without reason, I must admit. When we met again, I was clinging to the torrid affair we had at a time when neither of us was mature enough to face up to it.* His thoughts went way back to when he had first arrived in England.

Even Devon had more guts than I had to see the reality of falling in love with a white girl. He stuck with Rose and now they are happily married with three beautiful children. BJ sighed and leaned back with his arms stretched above his head. *Emma and I could have been like that if I hadn't rejected the whole situation all those years ago. Still, what's done is done.*

He moved to make himself more comfortable, an action that wasn't lost on him. *That's it!* He silently told himself. *I have to be comfortable in re-thinking my future. My meeting again with Emma has made me think more logically about everything. She said we couldn't pick up where we left off and she was right. I have been so naïve in my insistence that we might rekindle our love.* He took a sip of his coffee and stood to look through the window at his quintessential English country garden and he smiled. *There is no doubt in my mind that I love Emma as the mother of my son and I would venture so far as to say she feels the same about me in being the father of her child. Daniel will always be there to maintain the link, a loving link, but not one that demands we marry or be together. I see that now. The fact that Emma hasn't called in the past three weeks tells me she is either still confused as she was when she left here, or she has decided she doesn't want to be with me and is too polite and kind to tell me in case she shatters my feelings again. Dear Emma. She is honest to a fault, but she wouldn't deliberately offend anybody. That I do know about her for sure. Now I must call Gracie.*

~ * ~

Wayne arrived at Emma's house soon after they had spoken on the phone. When she opened the door to him, she initiated a hug. "I have missed this," she admitted.

"Me too," Wayne told her. "Are we friends again?" he asked with a smile.

She nodded. "Glass of wine?" she asked. "Let's sit in the kitchen so I can keep an eye on dinner while it cooks."

Wayne laughed. "What is this sitting in the kitchen while we talk? Is it an English thing?"

"I don't think so," Emma told him. "I'm sure every housewife sits in the kitchen if there is something cooking..." She paused and nudged him playfully. "Did you hear what I said? Something cooking? Well, there just might be something more than dinner on the agenda."

Wayne looked at her wide-eyed. "What are you suggesting, Miss Williams?"

Emma was shocked. "Oh, blimey! I didn't mean that," she said, her cheeks glowing like hot coals. "I meant there's a lot of discussion on the cards..."

Wayne took her hand and looked into her eyes. "Don't worry, Em. We're on the same page. I was just joking."

"Phew!" she breathed, "But I do have a lot to explain and I think I need another glass of wine to fortify me."

"Coming right up," Wayne said as he took the bottle of red and poured them both a generous glass of Lambrusco. "This is light enough for us to drink without becoming inebriated," he added.

"It is," Emma agreed as they sat at the breakfast bar facing each other. "First of all, please tell me how you are faring after the finalising of your divorce."

"That's easy, "Wayne declared. "My worries are over and while I'm here at the moment, I do have to go back to Vancouver to organise the big move."

"So you're still sure you want to live here?" Emma asked. "I mean, it's a massive step to take."

"From Vancouver to Kingston, yeah, well, just short of three thousand three hundred and fifty miles, but I think my legs are long enough to take that step!" he joked.

Emma smiled. "Don't joke about it, Wayne. When you hear what I have to say, you might change your mind."

"I won't," Wayne assured her. "My mind is made up, whatever you have to say."

"Okay," she said. "I quite like the sound of that. Now where shall I begin?"

"At the beginning, I presume."

Emma slowly shook her head and smiled in acceptance of his light-heartedness. "When I was at the degree ceremony, I was shocked when BJ arrived and sat next to me." She told Wayne the whole story, including her confusion and later the realisation that there was absolutely no way she could pick up with BJ where they left off. "My thoughts were of you constantly. I recalled the comfort I felt in your arms, the thrill of your kisses and although I had experienced all that with BJ in the past, I knew I had changed, *we* had changed and I realised the magic is not with BJ anymore. It is with you. I have to say, though, I shall always love BJ as the father of my son and we'll always have that connection. I'm trusting that when he has seriously thought about his situation, he will come to a similar conclusion. I'm hoping he'll marry his girlfriend whom he has kept dangling on a string for a few years. He has—no, change that—*we*—that is BJ and I, have to accept all we had, has gone. We have different paths to take now."

"Oh, Emma," Wayne said quietly. "Do you really think we could be together for the rest of our lives?"

She shrugged. "How can I answer that question, Wayne? We both know that things happen in life, but I'm willing to give it a try if you think you are ready to take on this opinionated, self-destructive woman." She laughed. "I might drive you to distraction!"

"It's a distraction I will enjoy," he told her. "Just so long as we weather all the storms together."

After dinner, they snuggled on the sofa and watched *The Odd Couple* on television. "Do you think people will describe us as an odd couple?" Emma asked as they laughed at the antics of Oscar and Felix coming to terms with their differing views on everything.

"I don't think so," Wayne replied confidently. "I think we are well suited."

Suddenly and without warning, Emma sat up and turned to the man she knew she could love, a forever kind of love she felt in the deepest recesses of her soul. She kissed him tenderly, passionately. "Stay with me tonight," she urged.

"Are you sure?" Wayne whispered.

She nodded and they kissed again, this time allowing their passion to take over as they went to her bedroom.

Twenty-four

Emma called BJ with renewed confidence. "Hi," she said. "How are you?"

"I'm good, thanks, Emma," he replied. "What took you so long?"

Emma looked at the phone in her hand, her eyes wide with astonishment. "I have only been home for just over three weeks and I told you I would call when I had settled in. I had to work the day after I got back. I do have a life to lead, BJ."

"No need to get on your high horse, Emma," he protested. "I just thought you would call sooner, that's all. Anyway, what's happening in your world?"

Emma pondered on the question before she answered. *How much do I tell BJ at this juncture?* "How are you and Gracie going?" she asked cautiously, trying to steer the conversation to be about BJ, not her. "Have you proposed yet?"

"Funny you should ask that," he said.

"You have?"

"Actually, I haven't, not yet, but I intend to when I see her at the weekend."

"Well done, BJ. Congratulations in advance. I hope you will be very happy," she told him. "I'm happy for you, truly happy."

BJ laughed. "I have you to thank for my change of heart," he revealed. "In a roundabout way, you made me see sense. I'll always love you, Emma. You are the mother of my son, and it took me a while to work out that the way I love you and the way I love Gracie are different. Gracie's love is the one constant I have in my life. When you left, I realised my hopes of rekindling our relationship were built on memories of what we had, not what is between us now. Thank you for injecting some wisdom into the equation."

"Don't thank me, BJ," Emma responded. "I know I made your life miserable when I was there. I allowed myself to get tied up with illogical feelings and everybody suffered for it. Poor Daniel got it in the neck."

"Did he?" BJ asked. "I didn't know about that. He didn't say anything to me, but I know you told him about Gracie,"

"Sorry if it was a secret, BJ."

"I guess it was then, but now I can shout it to the world," he said happily. "But not until I've actually done the deed." He laughed. "Why couldn't we have talked like this a few weeks ago?"

"That's easy," Emma admitted. "My irrational behaviour affected everybody's judgement. You and I had a very complicated romance, BJ. I'm sure you don't need me to tell you that. It was something we didn't allow to take its natural course. When you find somebody who makes it easy to follow your heart, it becomes a natural progression, like you and Gracie." She paused. "And Wayne and me..."

BJ's gasp was audible over the phone. "You and who?"

"Wayne," she repeated. "I actually met him in London during the war."

"And you caught up again in Jamaica?"

"Well yes, but not until a few months ago. He was visiting an old air force buddy," she explained. "We bumped into each other coming out of the cinema and he actually recognised me after thirty years! I have to be flattered with that. It's a long story, but we caught up and now we're a couple."

"Did you meet up with him before you came over here?" BJ asked, not hiding his surprise.

"I did, but I hadn't told anybody until Daniel and I were in The Lakes and I explained why I was so confused."

"So Daniel knew why you were so confused and you didn't think to tell me?" he complained.

"I didn't think I should bring him into the mix. Seeing you so unexpectedly brought back all the lovely memories of when we were together, but then, as I told you before, our romance caused me so much heartache and that in itself told me I shouldn't be living in the past. Wayne and I started as friends and our love for each other developed slowly. It is the mature love I tried to explain to you when I was over there, not the urgent passion that consumed you and me every time we were together."

"But you didn't tell me about him, Emma. Why?"

"Because when Gracie turned up that Saturday afternoon and I saw how much she was in love with you, I felt telling you about Wayne would have looked like tit for tat."

"How do you mean, tit for tat?" he asked, still amazed at what he was hearing.

"It would have sounded like a playground scrap..." She mimicked children's voices. "*If you have a girlfriend, then I can have a boyfriend. What's good for the goose is good for the gander etc, etc, etc.* I didn't want to cheapen both our relationships like that," she expounded. "We are better than that, BJ."

"I know that, Miss Emma." He laughed in his recollection of annoying Emma when he first arrived in England.

Emma laughed with him. "Less of the Miss Emma nonsense," she scolded playfully. "I'm glad we've cleared up our differences, BJ. I'll always love you in a father-of-my-child kind of way. Be sure you explain all that to Gracie. I hope she will understand, but if she loves you as I think she does, she'll be delighted to have you all to herself at last."

"Thanks, Emma," he concluded. "You be happy and I'll be happy, too."

Epilogue

The Robards and the Johnsons were both invited to the marriage of Daniel Williams-Johnson and Alison Jean Macdonald at The Royal College of Physicians in the centre of Edinburgh on Saturday, the second of August 1975. It was a lavish affair for the only daughter of Stuart and Isla Macdonald and the venue appropriate for the young couple who had not adhered to any religious preference.

"Daniel and Alison met at Birmingham University in 1968 and only allowed themselves to fall in love properly after they qualified..." words that were the introduction to the best man's speech during the reception, the best man being Lenny Bolton, husband of Alexa Bolton née Papadakis, both members of the Birmingham Seven, duly called because of the close and lasting friendships they had formed during the three years they were at university together.

"Alison was Dan's bodyguard..." Laughter echoed around the room as everybody noted the slender figure of Alison and the larger frame of her new husband. "I'm not suggesting you aren't tough, Dan, but I still have this picture of Alison standing up to some guy in the common room, telling him to show some humility and calling him an ignorant bastard..."

There were gasps all around the room, but everybody laughed, even Stuart and Isla, whose expressions were wide-eyed, but no offence was taken.

Daniel grinned. "That's my girl," he said and gave Alison a kiss on the cheek.

After many more mildly embarrassing stories of Daniel's time in Birmingham, like the first and only time Lenny had seen him the worse for wear in drinking too much, and having to walk back to halls in his stocking feet when he lost his shoes at the swimming pool...

"I found those shoes back in my wardrobe the following morning," Daniel added. "I wonder who put them there."

"Confession time," came a voice from the table at the back of the room. "I think it might have been me."

"Ah, now you decide to own up, Doctor Tom. Shame on you!"

Laughter again echoed round the room and then Lenny became more serious. "Dan is one of my closest friends, along with the rest of the motley crew on that back table. He is honest, trustworthy and loyal, so I know he will make an excellent husband and father."

"Is there something we should know?" BJ asked from his place in front of the happy couple.

"No, Dad," Daniel assured him. "You'll just have to wait a while longer for the pitter-patter of tiny feet."

"I'm happy with that," BJ replied.

"Me too," Emma added and then whispered in Wayne's ear. "At least they have waited until they are married. More than I did."

"All in the past, darling," he whispered back. "Just look at that fine young man. You should be very proud."

"I am," she said quietly.

As they all raised their glasses to the bride and groom, BJ smiled across at Emma and said, "To you, Emma. Thanks to you, we have a wonderful son, a remarkable young man and I shall be eternally grateful."

Wayne and Gracie raised their glasses in Emma's direction. "To Emma," they said in unison.

Meet Vera Berry Burrows

Vera Berry-Burrows is a UK-born former teacher of English Language and Literature, living in Queensland, Australia with former journalist husband, Alan. She has a son and two grandsons living in the UK. She has been writing for a number of years and has had numerous non-fiction articles published in the UK and in Australia. She was educated at Farnworth Grammar School in Lancashire, trained as a teacher at St Katharine's College, Liverpool and gained a Bachelor of Arts degree with the Open University, UK. Since she took early retirement in 1994 having been in the teaching profession for thirty-one years, writing has become her compulsive hobby.

Other Works From The Pen Of Vera Berry Burrows

Tomorrow Never Comes - Relationships seriously affect the lives of a controlling mother, Nell Winston and her rebellious son, Joel, until the elusive tomorrows make all the earth-shattering yesterdays worthwhile.

Regarding Kimberley - Kimberley Mason unwittingly unearths a thirty-year-old dark secret kept by her parents when she forms links with a theatrical agency in Sydney, Australia.

Connections – Connections for better or worse, made by Jane O'Connell after divorce, completely disrupt her life, both shattering and illuminating her existence with unexpected consequences.

Family Matters - In war-torn Britain, John Hawthorne and three daughters, Meg, Patty and Abigail, rally forth on the battlefield of their own shattered lives.

My Name is Aphrodite - Rodi Bartlett's worldwide search for her father is relentless, because she knows that somebody somewhere made her from love.

Dare to Dream - Leaving an orphanage upbringing behind, two teenage girls need to learn how to survive in a world thus far alien to them.

Payback - Julietta's holiday becomes a nightmare when she is swept up in the frenzy of other people's abhorrent need for revenge.

Skin Deep - Emma Williams and BJ Johnson fall madly in love, completely aware that their relationship will not be readily accepted by a post-war prejudiced society.

Letter to Our Readers

Enjoy this book?

You can make a difference

As an independent publisher, Wings ePress, Inc. does not have the financial clout of the large New York publishers. We can't afford large magazine spreads or subway posters to tell people about our quality books.

But we do have something much more effective and powerful than ads. We have a large base of loyal readers.

Honest reviews help bring the attention of new readers to our books.

If you enjoyed this book, we would appreciate it if you would spend a few minutes posting a review on the site where you purchased this book or on the Wings ePress, Inc. webpages at: https://wingsepress.com/

Thank You

Visit Our Website
For The Full Inventory
Of Quality Books:

Wings ePress, Inc

Quality trade paperbacks and downloads
in multiple formats,
in genres ranging from light romantic comedy to general
fiction and horror.
Wings has something for every reader's taste.
Visit the website, then bookmark it.
We add new titles each month!

Wings ePress Inc.
3000 N. Rock Road
Newton, KS 67114

www.ingramcontent.com/pod-product-compliance
Lightning Source LLC
Chambersburg PA
CBHW070915100726
47907CB00008B/2333